Good Riddance

MARG MCALISTER

BLUE GEM PUBLISHING

This edition published by Blue Gem Publishing in 2022.

Text and copyright © Marg McAlister 2015

Title: Good Riddance | Marg McAlister, author

ISBN: 978-1-922772-30-5 (Paperback edition)

ISBN: 978-0-9945205-2-4 (Ebook edition)

Cover Design by Annie Moril

V26032022

ALSO BY MARG McALISTER

SERIES 1
Good to Go

Georgie Be Good

Good Riddance

Up to No Good

In Good Hands

Too Good to be True

As Good as It Gets

Good Golly Miss Molly

Good Vibrations

A Rocking Good Christmas

SERIES 2
Good Intentions

A Good Result

No Good Reason

Good Fortune

CHAPTER 1

Tell me My Fortune

It wasn't often that a teenage boy found his way to Georgie's gypsy trailer to have his fortune told. In her experience, boys of that age usually stood around looking bored or wrestling with each other while their giggling girlfriends queued up to find out if they were going to be lucky in love. ("Not likely," Georgie felt like advising them, "unless you find a male who's a bit less of a Neanderthal.")

But kids were kids, and she could still remember the awkwardness of most of the boys she'd been to school with.

Now, here was another one.

Bending his head to walk through her door, tripping over his own feet on the way in, he was like a puppy that still had to grow into his paws. He stood there almost touching the ceiling and shoved his big hands into his pockets, looking everywhere but at her face. He looked as though he'd been put together out of a kit, with nothing quite fitting into place.

Reddish-brown hair flopped over his forehead, but his brows and lashes were black. A good-looking boy, but with some acne scarring on his cheeks that probably made him self-conscious. She put him at about seventeen.

"Hi," Georgie said. Looking at him, she was glad that she had put the little picket fence around her trailer, with a gate that held her sign, *"Please wait here for the next available appointment."* That way, she could leave the door open for some fresh air and still maintain confidentiality. Males as big as this one made her feel claustrophobic when the door was closed.

"Take a seat." She waved at the bench seat behind the table and then changed her mind. "No, wait. You've got such long legs; you might be more comfortable in a chair. Hang on."

She leaned out of the door and hauled up the folded camp chair that she kept handy for larger clients. Some were tall, like this boy. Others couldn't squeeze in between the table and the seat.

"Thanks." He took the chair from her, unfolded it, and sat down. He still looked awkward.

"It's a little cramped in here for taller people," Georgie said, sitting opposite him. "Can I get you a soda? Or water?"

He shook his head, still not meeting her eyes.

OK, thought Georgie. This was going to be a getting-blood-out-of-a-stone exercise.

"Have you been to a fortune-teller before?" she asked pleasantly.

That made him look at her—*glower* at her, more like. "No."

She gave a mental sigh but persisted. "So what brought you here today?"

"Entertainment," he said, his brown eyes challenging. "Isn't that what it says on the sign? That none of this is for real?"

Her carefully hand-lettered sign did indeed say *"For entertainment purposes only"*, to comply with the law… but what was he getting at?

"Fortune-telling can be entertainment, yes," she said carefully.

He seemed to struggle with himself and then forced a smile. "You have to say that, right? But you can tell the future. You advise people."

Georgie sat and looked at him for a moment,

trying to work out his agenda. Was this a boy who needed help but was putting on an aggressive front to hide his embarrassment? Or was he trying to bait her?

"People ask me questions," she said finally, "and I do my best to answer them. You have to understand that I don't base what I say on facts. How could I? I don't know the people who come to me. I don't know you. I have no idea why I know some of the things I do, and that's why I class it as entertainment." She shrugged. "Make of it what you will… just remember that in the end, we all have to make our own decisions."

"What if I don't agree with what you say?" His Adam's apple moved convulsively as he swallowed. "What if I think it's all rubbish and refuse to pay you?"

Then I'd recommend that your mother give you a good spanking, she thought, but kept calm. Something was going on here.

"If you felt that strongly," she said, "then I'd let you go and write it off to experience. I'm here to help people, not to make their lives more difficult."

"Hah. So you admit it. How can you help people with problems if you can't see into the future?"

Georgie sighed. Did she need this? "What's your name?"

He set his jaw. "You should be able to see that in your crystal ball, shouldn't you?"

"It's possible," she said. "Give me a false name if you want to. I need to call you *something*."

"Anthony," he said.

Nick, Georgie heard, as clear as a bell. Out of the corner of her eye, she caught a wisp of white mist forming in her crystal ball. She ignored it, maintaining eye contact with the boy.

"Fine, Nick," she said. "Anthony it will be if that's what you prefer."

His eyes widened, and his lips parted in surprise. "How did you do that?"

"Lucky guess," Georgie said dryly. "It couldn't possibly be the crystal ball. Tell me why you're here, *Anthony*."

"Well, if you know what it is, there's no point," he said sulkily. "Just go ahead and tell me my fortune."

"You were a lovely baby," Georgie said. Probably true, she thought. He was good-looking now; he was undoubtedly adorable then. "You had your mother in the palm of your hand. Whatever you wanted, you got. Which probably accounts for your sad lack of manners now." She was on a roll. "In high school, you had to decide between football and basketball, and football it was. If you'd stuck with basketball, you would have been a Shaq O'Neal type, but you decided you could use your weight to more advantage on the football field. You're doing OK, but you get into trouble now and then when you skip training."

He scowled when she got to the bit about bad manners but locked his eyes on to hers when she talked about football and basketball.

"You're guessing again," he said, with a shade less certainty in his voice.

"I could well be," she agreed. "I could be using native intelligence, too, seeing you're wearing a football jersey under that jacket. And with your attitude, it's likely that you would skip training and have arguments with the coach."

He sat back and folded his arms, daring her to go on.

"Are you feeling entertained yet?" she inquired sweetly.

"Tell me some more."

"Tell me some more, *please*, Georgie."

"You're not my mother."

"You don't know how glad that makes me feel."

His brows lowered, and just as Georgie was fully expecting him to get up and leave, he bit out, "*Please* tell me some more."

In her mind, Rosa's unmistakable voice croaked, *"Tell him his mother's mad at him because he forgot to feed Rusty."*

Startled, Georgie directed her gaze down at the crystal ball. Her great grandmother couldn't give her any information two weeks ago when a customer was facing arrest on a trumped-up charge, but she could show up now to talk about this kid needing to feed his *dog*?

Right, she thought. One phone call to Rosa coming up.

"Well?" he said, watching her narrowly.

Georgie sat back and folded her arms. "Your mother's mad at you because you forgot to feed Rusty."

His face changed. "You've been talking to my mother. Haven't you?"

"Anthony, I—"

"It's *Nick*."

"Nick, I've never met your mother."

"Liar," he said. "She was here yesterday and the day before. She's been telling you all about me, and you recognized me as soon as I walked in, didn't you? About how I had to choose between football and basketball? That's how you knew my name and my dog's name."

He shoved the chair back and stood up. "You're a fake. People like you shouldn't be taking people's money. And I'm not paying you."

With that, he whirled and stamped down the steps of her trailer, making it shake.

Georgie returned her gaze to the crystal ball, now innocent of any mist. Looking cheerful, it reflected a yellow beam of light angling in from one of the stained glass windows.

"Well, that went well," she said, drumming her fingers on the table.

CHAPTER 2

He's Toast

Layla kept an eye out for her, and when Georgie followed Nick/Anthony down the steps of the trailer, she waved her over. "I've made lunch! Come and see my new table setting!"

Layla liked nothing better than to switch her dinnerware and tablecloths around, delighting in the effect of something new. Everything was in pastel shades, with color names like Pink Chablis and Ice Blue and Frosted Apricot.

Today they were lunching outside, taking advantage of the mild weather, and Layla had draped a tablecloth with big pink cabbage roses on it over the outdoor setting. Dainty sandwiches were arranged on a pink plate with scalloped edges, and near it sat a new teapot in palest green, with tiny sprigs of pink blossoms around the base. The lid was matching pink, and the delicate cups echoed the colors.

"Where did you get that?" Fascinated, Georgie lifted the teapot and peered at it. "It's gorgeous!"

"Bought it at the retro rally from someone who's buying a new trailer in different colors. Isn't it great?"

"And look at you." Hands on hips, Georgie surveyed Layla's pink gingham apron, ridged with white eyelet lace, tied in a saucy bow at the back over her white shorts.

"I haven't dressed up for three days," Layla pointed out. "I was getting withdrawal symptoms. I bought this from the same person. She's going all bright blue and white next time." Then she took a second look at Georgie and pushed her giant sunglasses with heart-shaped lenses high on her forehead. "You're looking a bit strained. Difficult client?"

"You could say that." Georgie sank into a chair and chose a chicken and lettuce triangle. "Mmmm. Yum. New dressing?"

"Apricot sauce." Layla poured Earl Grey tea and pushed the cup and saucer towards her. "Here.

Try this. And tell me what's wrong. Anything you can talk about?"

Georgie tipped her head on one side and thought about it. How could you describe Nick/Anthony? A teenage kid with a chip on his shoulder about fortune-tellers. Man, she got some weird customers at times.

"A teenage boy," she said, "grown too big for his body, you know the look? Big and gangly at the same time. He wanted to be," she drew quote marks in the air with her fingers, "*entertained*." But when I gave him some information, he said it was because his mother had told me all about him. His *mother*. As if."

"I saw him leave," Layla said. "It's a wonder he fit in the trailer. And when, exactly, are you supposed to have seen his mother?"

Georgie licked a trickle of apricot sauce off her fingers and took a sip of the Earl Grey, and then closed her eyes in appreciation. "Mmm, you bought the kind with the flowers in it, didn't you?"

"Organic bergamot oil and blue cornflowers. Cost a bomb."

"This kid," Georgie said, "said his mother had been to see me twice this week. I think I know which one she was. Kind of an alternative type."

"If someone came twice, I guess you'd remember."

"I have my groupies," said Georgie primly, putting her nose in the air. "Lots of people come back for a second and third reading. One came every day last week." She cast her mind back. "This kid's mother, if she's the one I'm thinking of, dressed in layers. You know, three different tops, skirt and loose scarf." She snapped her fingers. "Katherine. That was her name."

"And did she talk about the kid?"

"Only in passing. Didn't mention his name—or the dog's—despite what he says. And guess who popped into the reading today, floating around in my crystal ball? Rosa." Georgie rolled her eyes. "And what did she tell me? That he should remember to feed his *dog*. Would she help me out when I needed her a few weeks ago, with poor Sarah and James? Oh no, not a whisper. But she butted in today. Go figure."

"Rosa sent a message? She only does that if you should be paying attention."

"And yet, she rarely tells me anything useful. Just pops in with something cryptic or to poke at me."

"Still." Layla swiped a second triangle of bread. "These are really good. If I were not bursting out of my shorts, I'd have made more." She demolished it in two bites and went on, "She's clearly sending you a message about more than the dog. I must meet your great-grandmother one day. She sounds interesting."

"She is that," Georgie agreed wryly. "I'm going to phone her later. I haven't spoken with her in person since she told me to consult the crystal ball at the end of the RV Expo three months ago. And look where that got me." She swept an arm around. "Sitting in LA wondering why this teenage kid has it in for me."

"You also prevented Kaylene from losing most of her savings to a con man in Dayton," Layla reminded her, "and saved young Izzie's life. That's pretty special."

"Even more special," Georgie said, "Is that I ended up with a Crystal Ball Investigation Team." She pointed at Layla with mock sternness. "So perhaps my team had better put their heads together and figure out what young Nick wants."

Layla grinned. "Are you saying we're not pulling our weight?"

"Not at all," Georgie said serenely. "You've only just found out. Now you can nudge the rest of the team into action."

"Nudge them yourself." Layla nodded behind her. "Here comes Tammy, with your favorite brother. And by the look on her face, Jerry is about to dump something else on you."

Oh good. The perfect end to her morning.

Georgie turned and sent Tammy a sunny smile, which wasn't hard because Tammy was one of her favorite people, even if her taste in men was incomprehensible. Today she looked as if she were about to go sailing, dressed in a smart navy blouse with a loose rolled white collar tied in a flirty bow and four large white buttons emphasizing the trim hips of her bright red shorts. Her blonde hair was still in the Marilyn Monroe waves she had adopted for the recent retro rally.

"Morning, Tams."

"Hi Georgie, Layla." She leaned over and examined the new teapot. "Ooh! Look at this. This gives me an idea for the vintage trailer display back at Elkhart. Where can I get one of these? Jerry, this is exactly what I was talking about this morning."

Jerry cast a cursory look at the flower-sprigged teapot. "Yeah, great. Whatever you want, Tams. You'll have it looking great. Just great."

She exchanged a look with Layla and turned to look at Jerry. "One too many 'greats' there. One day I'll adjust to the fact that you have no appreciation for vintage."

"Better get used to it," Georgie advised her. "If your RV doesn't have four slides, a party lounge, and a bar, it doesn't rate."

"Georgie, be good," Jerry reprimanded her. "You know I'm committed to growing all divisions of this business. Which brings me to a matter I needed to discuss with you." He cast her a wary look. "Now, hear me out before you start carrying on."

Tammy sat back, crossed her knees, and started swinging one perfect leg. Then she folded her arms and turned her head towards Jerry. They couldn't see her eyes behind her red-framed cats-eye sunglasses, and her face looked perfectly composed, but Jerry visibly gulped. "I've already had Tammy in my ear about this, but my mind's made up."

This didn't sound good. Georgie eyed him warningly. "Your mind is made up?"

"When you decided to give up managing vintage trailers to take to the road, it became my responsibility. So yeah, my mind is made up."

Tammy said nothing, but her leg swung faster.

"I thought Tammy was managing it now?"

"She's a great help, of course. But Tams hasn't

got the big picture view of the business that I have." He rushed on. "We're leaving vintage trailers at the RV Empire, as I promised, but we're shuffling things around a little. Now, I've agreed to relocate a large section of truck campers and BOVs to the new premises—and that was purely because you were so against moving vintage there, Georgie—but Dad needs the vintage space for his new Customer Care facility. So we're just making a little sideways move, and vintage will be in that nice quiet little corner behind the main workshop."

Georgie stared at him. He turned on his most charming Jerry smile, the one accompanied by sparkling eyes and one deep dimple. "See?" he said. "Nothing terrible at all. And Tams has these great ideas for picket fences and flowers, and your retro people will come in *droves*."

Tammy re-crossed her arms and kept staring in his direction through her impenetrable sunglasses.

He sat back, maintaining the practiced smile. "Dad's really happy with the way vintage sales are going. You girls are nailing it."

Georgie pictured herself nailing Jerry to a wall. Right at the front of Johnny B. Goode's RV Empire, where he could serve as a warning to others.

"No," she said.

The smile almost slipped, but Jerry regrouped. "What do you mean, no?"

"I mean no. *No.*"

"Well, with all due respect, Georgie, I wasn't asking for permission. I'm just doing you the courtesy of keeping you informed."

Layla's eyes widened. Tammy's leg stopped jigging.

Georgie reached over and took another chicken-and-lettuce triangle and nibbled at it, regarding Jerry thoughtfully. What he was suggesting probably was a practical way to reorganize the available space; she could see that. The only problem was that it was just *one* way, and his arrogance in completely ignoring her feelings—and Tammy's—about vintage trailers took her breath away.

Nobody was putting her vintage trailers in a corner.

The silence grew.

Georgie took her time finishing her sandwich and then said, "What do you think, Tammy?"

Tammy pushed her sunglasses down her nose with her fingertip and gazed steadily over the top at Jerry. "I would prefer to have the vintage trailers where they catch the eye of visitors as soon as they drive in. They're cheerful and colorful, and they put people in a good mood, even if they're there to look at some other kind of RV." She glanced at Georgie. "Move the 5th Wheels across a little, juggle the truck campers, and rotate the pre-loved trailers between their present spot and the corner behind the workshop."

With her trained designer's eye, Georgie could instantly picture the effect when people drove in. Tammy was untrained but a natural. She nodded approvingly. "And you shared this with Jerry?"

"I started to," Tammy said, her voice cool. "But Jerry was so enthusiastic about this latest plan that he wanted to get over here and tell you right away. I did attempt to speak with him, but he was too caught up in his own plans."

Jerry started to look unhappy. "Now, girls, it's not that big of a deal. Vintage and retro people, they'll go looking for the trailers wherever you put them. I've already made a huge compromise in agreeing to move truck campers and BOVs off-site."

Layla, quiet until now, butted in. "Will somebody tell me what the heck a "BOV" is?"

"Bug-Out Vehicle," said Tammy. "You know, for preppers." She pushed her sunglasses back over her eyes. "Which is Jerry's pet interest, along with any other kind of extreme RV. Just as vintage trailers is *my* pet interest, and Georgie's."

Her message was clear.

Tammy stood up. She put her hands on her hips and stared at Jerry, a curvy gorgeous blonde in her 50s shorts and blouse.

He stared back, a hint of panic in the back of his eyes.

"If you do this, Jerry," said Tammy, "I'm going to get a teeny bit mad."

She reached over, and he flinched, but she just ran a hand gently over his hair before patting him on the cheek.

Then she walked off. All three watched her, her trim bottom swinging in the red shorts and her blonde hair bouncing.

Georgie looked at Jerry.

He kept his eyes on Tammy until she climbed the steps of her new retro trailer and disappeared and then cleared his throat and stood up.

"I'll give it more thought," he said, not meeting Georgie's eyes, and walked off after Tammy.

"He's toast," Layla said complacently. "More tea?"

CHAPTER 3

Super Secret Spy

The weather at their current RV park near Santa Monica was perfect, and that was why Georgie told herself that she needed more summer clothes. That decision, she admitted to herself, might have had something to with being around the retro trailer set with their never-ending delight in vintage fashions. Since she had already bought half of Mags' stock for her gypsy persona, Georgie decided some casual 50s outfits might be nice. After all, as she said to Layla, she was part of the road team for *all* of the vintage division, not just gypsy trailers, right?

"Yeah, right," Layla had responded. "Like you need an excuse."

The next step was to find somewhere to stash

her newfound finery. Happily, the new male in her life, Scott, had returned from a short stint relieving a campground host at an RV park near LA and didn't require much persuasion to go hunting for storage options for Georgie's 4WD. Now Georgie and Layla were basking in the sun, watching him install a set of slide-out drawers in the back of the truck.

"Very useful, having a boyfriend who has a full set of handyman tools with him," Layla observed, sprawled in Georgie's camp chair with her feet up on a box of sales brochures. "What did you say he did back in Australia?"

Georgie, sitting on the steps of her trailer pointing her foot and turning it this way and that to admire her new two-toned flats that went with her red gingham playsuit, said absently, "Something like a park ranger, I think. National parks? Fisheries? He has a degree in something to do with the environment."

"*He* can hear you, you know," Scott said without turning around, sliding a drawer in and out to test it. "He has a Bachelor of Environmental Science. Which qualifies him to work in pretty much any environment." He paused to make an adjustment and tried it again. "Including aquaculture and forests." He stood back to survey his work. "There you go. All done. If you can refrain from buying any more clothes, this should do you."

"Can't promise that," Georgie said, exchanging a grin with Layla. She sprang up and walked over to check his handiwork. "Very nice. Thank you. That will get you all kinds of favors."

"Dangerous words, when I've been away for ten days," Scott said, tipping up her chin and planting a kiss on her lips. "Your place or mine tonight?"

"Mine," she decided. "I'll cook dinner."

Layla sighed, watching them. "I have got to find a man. You've got Scott. Tammy has Jerry. I feel deprived. Didn't you say that I'd find him in LA?"

"I think I said you'd *commit* to someone in California," Georgie remembered from the one reading she had done for Layla. "But I couldn't tell when. Do you want another reading?"

Scott slung a companionable arm around Georgie. "I could do a card reading too. See if we agree."

Layla eyed him doubtfully. "I thought your mother was the one who did horoscopes?"

"She is, but you'd be surprised at how much I've picked up over the years."

Georgie wasn't surprised at all. She still felt

that Scott knew a lot more about her—and the future—than he was letting on. No doubt she'd find out one day if her suspicions were correct. Meanwhile, she didn't mind a bit of mystery in her life.

Other than what she had thrown at her via the crystal ball.

Thinking of the crystal ball made her realize that it was getting late, and her afternoon clients would be turning up soon.

"I'd better go and change," she said, looking regretfully down at the playsuit. "This is comfort-able. And cool."

"Stay in it, then," suggested Scott.

They both just looked at him and then at each other, exchanging a faint smile.

He got the message. "Oh right, you have to stay in character. Well, I'm sure you have something comfortable and cool somewhere in the half a ton of stuff you bought from Mags." Scott eyed the piles of colorful clothes stacked up, ready to put in the new drawers.

Georgie put her hands on her hips. "And your point is?"

"Nothing," Scott said hastily. "It's all good. You need clothes. And now you have drawers to keep them in." He turned to gather his tools. "I'll just pack up and let you get on with it."

Georgie grinned. "Just kidding, Scott." She eyed the piles of clothes and chose a pink and brown striped skirt and a cream drawstring blouse. Then she added a lacy rust-colored shawl to tie around her waist and finally snatched up a bright headscarf that toned with everything else.

Gypsy-ish and still comfortable.

This was a great life.

She stayed in that happy frame of mind for most of the afternoon, right up until her last appointment, when Nick turned up again.

Georgie sighed. "Hello, Nick. You're back."

"I suppose you're going to turn me away after yesterday," he said. Standing at the bottom of the three steps that led up to her door, he was almost at eye-level. Today he was dressed in a nondescript pair of jeans and a cotton shirt, with no football jersey to give him away. He had a notebook and a pen crammed into his shirt pocket.

"I'm not going to spend more time with you just to have you insult me if that's what you mean."

Georgie leaned against the doorframe and folded her arms. "Be prepared to take it seriously or forget it."

His eyes went to the sign on the gate with her current rates and the words *"For entertainment purposes only."* He arched an eyebrow.

"That's the deal," Georgie said, unmoved. "And pay upfront."

"Jeez." Looking affronted, he pulled out his wallet and extracted a twenty-dollar bill, holding it out to her. "I'd better hear more than my dog's name today, then."

Georgie still didn't invite him in. "You take what comes. If you don't want to be *entertained*, then go away."

"Jeez," he said again but stayed where he was. "All right, then." He motioned for her to take the twenty.

"One more thing. Why are you here if you don't believe in all this? Yesterday you called me a fake."

He said nothing for a moment, holding her gaze, and then muttered, "I might need help with something."

Still in two minds about whether to let him in, Georgie returned his stare and concentrated on trying to figure out what he was thinking. She had no immediate revelations but no sense that he was a threat, either, so she took the twenty and beckoned him inside. "Bring that chair with you."

He toted the chair up the steps and settled himself at the table. His eyes went immediately to the crystal ball.

Georgie filled two glasses with water and set them on the table, and made herself comfortable on the bench seat. She adjusted her headscarf, flicked her hair back over her shoulders, and looked at him. "Ready?"

"Yes." He pulled the notebook and pen out of his pocket and clicked the pen top. "I might take some notes. Is that okay?"

"It's rare for me to come up with so much information that anyone needs to take notes," Georgie said, "but feel free."

He flipped to the first page in the notepad and wrote the date and time.

"Okay. How did you get to be a gypsy fortune teller?" He looked at her expectantly.

"Excuse me?" Georgie's eyebrows flew up. "I didn't realize this was an interview."

"I'm just trying to establish your bona fides," he explained.

"Says it all on the sign outside. Eighth generation gypsy. It's in the family genes." She smiled at him, amused. "Did you think that I had been to college to study this?"

"Well, when did you start? And why *are* you telling fortunes? Did you ever have any other kind of job?"

Georgie blinked. Oh, for Pete's sake. "I started three months ago; I'm doing it because I feel as though I should, and yes, I have a degree in design. And my family sells RVs. Is that enough for you, O Doubtful One? Or should I produce a certificate or two?"

"No, that's all I needed to know." He scribbled in the notepad.

Georgie squinted and read it upside down. He had written: "Completely unqualified."

She folded her hands in front of her. "Is this a school project of some kind?"

Nick frowned. "No, it's for me. Does it make you uncomfortable that I'm questioning your credentials?"

Georgie was seized by an insane desire to laugh, but she managed to keep a straight face. "My "credentials" are an open book. Now, can we get on with this? You said I might be able to help you. How, exactly?"

Nick wouldn't meet her eyes again. "If you don't mind, I'll just ask a few more questions, and then I'll tell you how you can help."

"I've got a better idea," Georgie said testily. "I'll ask the questions, and we'll see if you're wasting my time again or not."

"In a minute," Nick said stubbornly. "How do you know that what you see is accurate?"

"Didn't we go through this yesterday?"

"But yesterday, I didn't take notes."

Georgie gave up. She had never met a kid like this one. "Fine. Fire away."

Nick went through a dozen questions, along the lines of: "What do you do if you're not sure of the answer?" and "Do you ever make things up because you think you can guess?" and other questions calculated, she assumed, to give him enough data to decide whether to believe her.

Finally, he nodded and put the pen down. "Okay. Now it's your turn. What do you see in my future?"

"Oh, besides the likelihood that I'll be throwing you down the steps with a heartfelt 'Good riddance'?" she said in honeyed tones.

"No. I mean it."

Georgie closed her eyes for a moment. Be calm, she told herself. Treat him like any other client.

She drew the crystal ball close to her and laid her hands on it, waiting to tune into its vibrations. Which, after facing a barrage of skeptical questions from Nick, sounded a very new-agey and flaky way to think about it, but she couldn't come up with a more accurate way to put it.

Don't you dare pop in now, Rosa, she sent as strongly as she could. She wanted to figure this one out for herself.

"What do you see?"

"Sssh." Tuning him out, she focused on how she might help. What had brought him to her?

Money, she thought—more flowing out than in.

"Are you having financial problems, Nick?"

"No."

The answer was too quick; the denial just a bit too strong. So, she'd hit a nerve there. Still letting part of her mind stay open to possibilities, Georgie thought it through.

Teenage boys and money. The first thing that came to mind was that he might be involved with drugs if money was short. What else? There was always the possibility of a stand-over merchant at school. But Nick was bigger than most kids, and he looked strong enough to hold his own. Probably not.

He played sport. Was that a connection? It was just high-school football; nobody would bet on it, so he wouldn't be taking bribes to throw a game.

She decided to let it go.

"How many are in your family, Nick?"

"How many do you think?"

She had no sense of a male around or any energy from siblings. "I think it's just you and your mother. You're the man of the house."

"You could have found that out from her."

"I could have, but I didn't. I haven't seen your mother since you were here yesterday."

"What about my football…?" He hesitated. "Will I ever play at the Superbowl?"

The answer came immediately, without her having to think, but she instinctively changed it from a flat 'no' to let him down gently. "I don't see that in your future. Sorry, Nick."

"Oh." His face fell. "What, just like that? There's no hope at all?"

"Not that I can see, but the future is never etched in stone." She was confident that he wouldn't, but he already seemed crushed enough.

"I would be delighted for you to prove me wrong."

"All right then." She could read the disappointment in his eyes, but he kept going. "What about college? Will I get an offer?"

Yes, the answer came to her with complete certainty. Football. "Yes, you *will* get a football scholarship." She grinned. "That could be conditional on your turning up to training more regularly."

"And my friend, Caleb? Will he get one too?"

"That I can't tell you. I'm attuned to you, not him."

She looked at her watch. "Time's up, Nick." He'd gone well over, but she didn't mind—until he stood up and held out the pen, resting on his upturned palm.

"See this?"

She looked at it and then looked up at him. "Your pen?"

"It's a recording device. I have video and audio of our session. Everything you said."

Georgie laughed. She couldn't help it. "You only had to ask. I let any of my clients record a session quite openly."

"Ah," he said, "but if I'd done that, you would

have been more careful about what you said, wouldn't you?"

"Not at all. It would have gone exactly the same way."

"I don't think so." He closed his fingers around the pen and picked up his notebook. "I still think you're a fraud, Georgie Goode. And I think this proves it. I'm going to be taking this to the police."

With an air of triumph, he made a dramatic exit.

Georgie sat staring after him, stunned.

Was this kid for real?

CHAPTER 4

Council of War

That night, Georgie had a council of war with her CBI team, recounting Nick's visit.

Tammy thought it was funny. Layla was open-mouthed. Scott just looked at her thoughtfully and rubbed the back of her hand. He seemed to know instinctively that although she was amused, she was also a little afraid.

"I think you're safe," he said to her. "You've made it clear to every client that it's principally for entertainment, haven't you?"

"Of course I have. It's on the sign, and I tell them as well. But, you know…" she sighed. "It's nudge nudge, wink wink, and 'can you tell me what will happen anyway?'"

"That's their problem, not yours," Tammy

pointed out. Her eyes were still bright with laughter. "Sorry, Georgie, I don't mean to take it lightly. It's just this boy—he's unbelievable! Like a cartoon character. It's as though he had made up his mind, and he's just out to catch you. He's like a vigilante."

Georgie nodded, breaking out in a reluctant smile. "He's not a very good spy. Imagine telling me that he had a hidden camera. What if I'd sent an enforcer after him to snatch it back?"

"Enforcer?" Scott looked around him. "You weren't thinking of me, were you?"

"I wasn't thinking of anyone. Honestly, I don't think I'll hear from him again."

They talked around the problem for another half hour, but with just 'possible financial trouble' as all she had picked up, they didn't have much to go on. Finally, Georgie sat back and held up a hand in a 'stop' motion. "Let's talk about something else. If the cops turn up at my door, then I'll deal with it. Otherwise, I'm just going to write young Nick off as a problem child."

"And a problem client," Layla pointed out.

"That too." Deliberately, Georgie changed the subject. "Tammy, I thought you were going back to Elkhart with Jerry today?"

There was a brief silence, and then she said coolly, "I *was*."

All eyes focused on her.

"I'm very fond of Jerry," she said. "You all know that."

They all nodded.

"And it's kinda fun using every weapon at my disposal to outwit him. I mean, half the time, he knows I'm doing it, and he teases me about it. He's not stupid."

"Far from it," Georgie agreed. "Do I hear a 'but' coming?"

"But," Tammy said, "every weapon includes more than sexy clothes—which I love wearing anyway—and sharing a laugh and willing to listen to his ideas about the business. It means I've got a brain too. Right?"

A chorus of 'rights' assured her than she did.

"It's not all about playing games. I know I'm right about where vintage trailers should go. *You* know I'm right. And deep down, I think Jerry knows I'm right, but he doesn't want to give in. He just doesn't want to lose. Because that's how he sees it."

They all waited.

"So I'm staying right here. I canceled the truck

to take my trailer back, and I'm letting Jerry dictate what happens to vintage back at Elkhart." She shrugged. "If it means more to him to stick to his guns and have his way than to weigh it up and take suggestions, well then…" She drew a finger across her throat.

"Wow," Georgie said. "I'm not sure whether that means you'll call it quits, or you plan to kill him."

Tammy nodded, but her bottom lip trembled. "Oh, Georgie. He can be stubborn and arrogant, but gorgeous and funny, too, and I love him."

"But you'd give him up." Georgie stood up and hugged her.

Tammy hugged her back and sniffled. "I can't live with a man who won't take me seriously."

"If he doesn't come back and apologize," said Georgie, "I'll be sending my enforcer after him." She shot a furious look at Scott. "Won't I, Scott?"

He tipped his head back and stared at the ceiling. "This is what happens when you get tangled up with a gypsy fortune-teller. Maybe it's time I went back to Australia."

The following day, Georgie left Scott in charge of any possible retro trailer inquiries while she headed off with Layla, Tammy, and Mags to what Tammy termed a 'girl fest'. This involved an extended morning tea on the Third Street Promenade and lively discussions about retro fashions related to interior design and clothes. With her fabulous line of gypsy and Boho clothing, Mags had traveled with them to Santa Monica and was full of ideas— one of which left Georgie stunned.

"You want to design a special label using *my* name?" Georgie shot a glance at Tammy. "Not sure how Jerry will react to that."

Mags looked at her as though she was kidding. "Georgie, whose name is associated with vintage and retro at the Johnny B: Good RV Empire? Who turned up at the Expo in a vintage gypsy trailer? Who is on the road all the time and hangs out with the retro crowd *and still has the family name?*" She opened both hands wide in a "this is obvious" gesture. "Your father has been playing the 'B. Goode' card ever since he started in the RV business. Every TV ad has some slogan. You and Jerry have appeared in countless 'this is a family business' ads—"

Georgie stopped her before she got on a roll.

"OK. OK, You're right. When I think about it, Dad will probably be relieved that I'm getting on board at last."

"Of course he will," said Tammy. "I've got to know him well over the past few months. He's always talking about his little Georgie girl. He'll be thrilled."

"Here's what I'm thinking," Mags said, pulling a bulging scrapbook out of a vast embroidered tote. "We'll talk about each line in detail later, but we'll go for different kinds of looks, but elements from each one will tie in with another." She glanced up. "You know the kind of thing: use the same scarf, but tie it in different ways; wear a blouse on the shoulder or off the shoulder. I've done some rough sketches for you."

Georgie, Layla, and Tammy leaned in close as she flipped through the scrapbook. She had put headers on each section: Traditional Gypsy, Wild Gypsy, Sexy Gypsy, Pretty Gypsy, and a few more. The pages were a riot of color and texture in themselves, with scraps of fabric and lace—rich velvets, slippery silks, delicate lace, samples of embroidery.

Mags' smile grew wider and wider at the chorus of 'wows' and 'I want it'. Finally, Georgie sat back looking dreamy. "It's so, so fantastic. My own clothing label. Oh, Mags."

"I'm glad you like it," she said, trying to look modest and failing. "I was so excited about it I could scarcely sleep. It's good for you and good for me. Your family name will help sell it, and my name as a designer will be out there."

Layla laughed. "Better get a bigger truck, Georgie. Poor Scott. More drawers to build."

"Actually," said Mags, "I realized that's going to be a problem for me, too. All my clothing line is stashed in my campervan, but I've got to sell that and buy something to tow my new gypsy trailer. And whatever I buy has to be fitted out so that I can transport the samples around."

They looked at each other, realizing that she was right.

"I've got an eBay store," Mags said. "But I need to carry a lot more stock with me since I'm on the road."

"This just keeps growing," Georgie said. She put her chin on her hand and frowned into her coffee cup, stirring the leftover froth absently. "We're going to need some help. Let me think."

She wanted it all to happen, but she didn't want to give up the joy of her gypsy lifestyle to go back to corporate concerns. She *couldn't* go back to working in an office. She was pretty sure that the others felt the same.

A very irritating thought kept surfacing. She tried to push it away and think of other options, but it just kept popping back up.

Jerry was the one who was so good at coordinating all this stuff. Jerry and Tammy together would be all over it.

Dammit.

She sighed and looked across the table at Tammy, who was, it turned out, looking at her.

"Are you thinking what I'm thinking?"

"I think I might be," Tammy said. "Jerry?"

"Jerry and you. Why now, just when you're not speaking? Anyway, I'm not going to make the first move. We'll see if he makes good. If he goes ahead with his stupid plan for relocating vintage," Georgie said firmly, "then it's war."

CHAPTER 5

A Surprise Visitor

The next day, when Georgie put out her sign to show that she was open for business, she found herself glancing around nervously to ensure that Nick wasn't waiting in the wings with a couple of rock-jawed cops.

"Relax," Scott said, putting a comforting hand on her shoulder. "You've got nothing to fear." He kept his voice low because there were two women waiting nearby. "I'm heading off with Mags to look at trucks and storage."

"I don't expect to be arrested," Georgie said, putting a brave face on it. Inside her, a small voice disagreed: *Yes, I do.*

"I don't expect you to be either, but Layla and Tammy are sticking around just in case Nick comes back to give you more trouble. Don't put up with it, Georgie."

"Okay. I won't."

"You're a shocking liar," Scott said, smiling. He dropped a kiss on her forehead. "Take care. Love the outfit, by the way."

Momentarily distracted, Georgie glanced down at her embroidered skirt and smoothed a hand down over the lacy shawl draped across one hip. "So do I. It's from Mags' Pretty Gypsy range." She had put the combination of soft fabrics and warm colors to make herself feel better, and it was working.

"Pretty indeed," Scott agreed and gave her another kiss for good measure.

He left, and she walked across to the waiting women, who were admiring the attractive picture formed by Layla and Tammy, gossiping outside Tammy's smart red and white retro trailer.

"Hi," Georgie greeted the women. Her gaze followed theirs. "Feel as though you've stepped back half a century?"

They both turned to her, smiling, and one said, "They look like they're having such a good time. I'd love a trailer like that."

"Easily done." Georgie grinned. "Those two

girls are our vintage road team. Go over and have a chat if you want to know more." She looked from one to the other. "Who do I see first?"

"Me," said the first woman. "I'm Steph. This is my friend Mia."

"They really wouldn't mind?" asked Mia, still looking across at Tammy.

"They'd love it. Go on over." Georgie caught Tammy's eye and waved and then pointed to Mia.

Tammy made 'come and join us' motions with a cheerful grin, and Mia trotted off happily.

"This is going to be fun," Steph said, following Georgie up the steps of her trailer. "I love fortune-tellers. A friend of mine told me about you. Are you here for long?" At Georgie's invitation, she slid into the seat behind the table and rubbed her hands together, looking around. "What a gorgeous trailer!" Her eyes moved up to where the sunlight was fractured into different colors through the stained glass. "Lucky you, living in this."

Georgie smiled as she slipped the black velvet cover off the crystal ball, already more relaxed with Steph's pleasure in her surroundings. This was just the kind of client she needed right now.

Both Steph and Mia turned out to be fun. Forty minutes later, she saw Mia out of the trailer and went down to welcome the third client for the morning. When she turned around, Georgie's heart sank.

It was Katherine, wearer of many layers, and if she was right, Nick's mother.

"Surprise, surprise!" Katherine trilled brightly. "I'm back again. I hope you're not tired of me!" Confident of her welcome, she moved towards the trailer.

"Not at all," Georgie said. "But… you've already been several times. I don't know how much more I can tell you."

Katherine brushed her off. "Let me be the judge of that. You told me things the second time that didn't come up in our first session, didn't you?" She followed Georgie inside and laid a twenty-dollar note on the table. "You should charge more, you know."

Georgie looked at the money, Nick's accusations echoing in her mind. "Katherine, this makes sixty dollars you've spent this week. Are you sure you want another reading?"

"Absolutely." She plunked herself down, her shapeless brown leather bag beside her.

Indecisive, George remained standing for a beat and then made up her mind.

"Your son is Nick, right?"

Katherine looked at her warily. "Yes."

"Did you know he came to see me the day after your last session?"

Katherine sighed. "I was hoping you hadn't made the connection between us, but I guess that was too much to expect. Last night he told me about both visits. I'm really sorry."

Georgie sat down. "It wasn't particularly nice having the police held over my head. Did he tell you he recorded the session?" Despite herself, a grin crept through. "On his secret video pen?"

"Yes, and after I watched it on his laptop, I told him if he went to the police, I'd never speak to him again." She risked a small smile. "Of course, I didn't mean it, but I would have been furious. I apologize for what he did."

"But *why*? Why is he so angry about all this?" Really, Georgie thought, forty dollars wasn't that much to spend on a reading. *Two* readings. Even today's taking it up to sixty dollars wasn't breaking the bank.

Nevertheless, she pushed the money back towards Katherine. "Let's not worry about this. Let's just talk."

Katherine flushed, refusing to touch it. "No, absolutely not. He's embarrassed me enough. He told me he refused even to pay for the first time and only paid for the second so he could get evidence!" She rolled her eyes. "*Evidence.* Who does he think he is, one of the CSI team?"

Georgie had to look away and cover a smile at that, thinking of her fledgling "Crystal Ball Investigation" team. "But why?" she persisted. "It just doesn't make sense, Katherine. Has he been ripped off by a fake psychic or something himself? Is that what it is?"

"No." She seemed to struggle with herself briefly and then shrugged. "It's... my sister. His aunt. His *favorite* aunt. She, um, got caught up with this online psychic and paid thousands of dollars before she ran out of cash."

Georgie relaxed. That would explain it. "So when he knew that you'd come to me twice, alarm bells started ringing? He thought you were going to do the same?"

"Yes." Katherine sat forward, nodding. "I'm sure that's what it was. But I told him that you were nothing like the other one, and he didn't need to worry."

"Okay." Georgie tapped her fingers on the table. Something just didn't sit right.

"Please?" Katherine looked uncertain. "I need to ask you about something."

"Of course." Georgie uncovered the crystal ball and rested her hands on it. This time she didn't form a question in her mind—nothing specific, anyway. She just thought of Nick and his mother and what she'd just learned about his aunt.

Instantly, she knew that Katherine was lying to her.

It was so odd the way this worked. She never knew from one minute to the next whether she would get a name, an image, or a sentence spoken in Great-Grandma Rosa's sardonic tones. This time, she got nothing but a feeling. No, a *certainty*.

Katherine was hiding something.

Georgie smiled across at her. "You said there was something you needed to ask me about."

"Yes." Katherine avoided Georgie's gaze, under the pretext of looking around the trailer in appreciation, tilting her head to look at the carving around the ceiling fixture. The flicker of candlelight enhanced the cozy atmosphere inside the trailer.

Finally, Katherine flicked a glance at Georgie again and then studied her bitten fingernails. "Am I in danger?"

"Are you in *danger*?" Surprised, Georgie blinked. Under her fingers, the crystal ball seemed to grow warmer.

"Is there someone…stalking me?" Katherine bit her lower lip.

Carefully, Georgie felt her way. "Do you feel that someone is doing that?"

"Kind of."

Kind of. What sort of answer was that? Georgie dug deeper, while on another level, she let herself be receptive to responses from the crystal ball. "Tell me why you think that."

"Nick and I live by ourselves. Just us and Rusty, our Pugzu."

A Pugzu… Georgie searched her memory and remembered that a Pugzu was a crossbreed, part pug, part shitzu. A small dog—not something that would frighten off too many intruders.

"We're in a small house," Katherine went on. "My husband died years ago, but we've managed to hang on to the house, although it's been a struggle at times."

Georgie was beginning to put it together. If

money was tight, then a football scholarship was essential to Nick. If life had been hard, he'd naturally be concerned about his mother falling victim to a fake psychic, just as his aunt had done.

"I don't tell everyone this because they wouldn't understand, but I know you will." Katherine took a deep breath. "I've had a message from beyond the veil…from my husband. He said I need to be careful, that someone is watching me. Someone who means me no good." Nervously, she shifted in her seat. "Can you tell me anything more?"

"Katherine, I'm not a medium. I can't communicate with people beyond the grave."

"No, no, that's not what I meant. I don't need you to do that. I just thought you might know who this person watching me might be."

Georgie's hands were growing very warm. She lifted them a fraction and glanced at the crystal ball. Sure enough, the inside was cloudy, but there were no images. No voices.

Nothing but a feeling.

"Katherine," she said, "are you saying that you…talk to your husband?"

"Not exactly. I don't talk to him. I use a medium to ask questions and get messages through. She's terrific."

The moment she spoke, Georgie realized two things.

One, that Katherine didn't have a sister who had paid out thousands to a fake psychic. That was Katherine herself.

Two, she was in danger of being defrauded again—by a charlatan who was pretending to convey messages from her husband.

Georgie listened as Katherine talked about her dead husband, empathizing with her loss. Several times, she tried to bring the conversation around to the medium, but Katherine was evasive.

There was nothing else for it. Georgie needed to see Nick.

"Katherine," she said towards the end of their session, leaning towards the other woman with a gentle smile, "I think it might be useful if I came to see you at home. Maybe I could pick up on it if someone is watching you. Would that be all right?"

Katherine was thrilled. "Really? That's fantastic! Today?"

"If you like." Might as well strike while the iron is hot, Georgie thought. Late afternoon might work. That should give Nick time to get home from school. "Say around four o'clock?"

"Four would be perfect," said Katherine. "By

that time, Nick will have been and gone. He usually comes home for a snack and then goes to the gym."

Perfect indeed, thought Georgie. She would get there an hour earlier to try to catch him.

A stakeout. Now she really felt like an investigator.

CHAPTER 6

Allies

Katherine's house was, as she had said, tiny. Talk about the worst house in the best street—it bore signs of having no man around to take care of it and no money to pay someone else to do it. Paint was peeling off the clapboard exterior, and the railing on the front steps was cracked.

The front lawn wasn't too bad—evidently, Nick could push a mower around—but the shrubs needed cutting back.

Georgie consulted her watch. Two fifty-three. She pushed the driver's seat back further and got comfortable.

She intended to keep an eye out for Nick, grab him before he went inside, and ask him a few pointed questions to see if her suspicions were correct. The worst that could happen, she reflected, was that she could look like an absolute idiot if he didn't turn up. Then she revised that.

No, the worst that could happen would be if Nick caused a scene in the street.

She unscrewed the top on a bottle of water and took a long drink. This was a lot more nerve-wracking than just doing a reading.

Fifteen minutes later, she decided that stake-outs were more boring than nerve-wracking. She should have brought Mags' gypsy fashion scrapbook.

Sighing, she Googled 'fake psychics' and read several websites outlining typical scams. Some scams were based on continuing consultations, with the fake psychic milking the victim for more and more money. Some relied more on volume: lots of people contacting them for short sessions.

Then a flash of movement in her side mirror made her glance up. Nick was slouching his way along the street towards her, his head down.

Georgie jumped out of the truck and moved around the front to block his way. "Nick?"

His head jerked up. When he realized who it was, he stopped short. His gaze whipped across to his house, and he scowled ferociously. "Have you been to see my mother? You're coming to the *house* now?"

"Not yet. I wanted to see you first."

"You can't talk me out of going to the cops," he said aggressively. "Don't even try."

"Nick, please. Just five minutes?"

He hesitated, torn. "I'm not my mother. You can't con me."

"I appreciate what you're doing for her, honestly. Just tell me one thing: do you have an aunt who lost thousands of dollars to a fake psychic?"

He stared at her as though she were crazy. "I don't have an aunt. Who told you that?"

"Your mother," Georgie said. "When she came to see me this morning. She said that's why you were giving me such a hard time."

He snorted. "What a joke. She's the one who lost thousands of dollars. And now she's ready to do it again, with you."

"Not with me," Georgie said, "but maybe with someone else." She took a deep breath. "If you work with me, we can catch them. Let the police know." Down by her side, she clenched her fingers into a fist. *Go on, agree, dammit.*

He stared at her and then glanced across at his house. She saw the indecision on his face and felt a pang of compassion. He was just a boy, trying to do the right thing…trying to protect his mother. It would have been hard, losing his father at a young age.

"I'm not the one, I promise you," Georgie said. "Work with me, and it won't cost you a thing. We might even be able to get some of your mother's money back."

Hearing herself speak, she was appalled. How could she promise that? She was as bad as anyone else who made promises they couldn't keep.

You can do it, said a strong voice in her mind.

"I can't promise you anything," she said, ignoring the voice. "But we can try."

"I don't know…"

"You can record everything I say to you," Georgie said. "I'm not hiding anything. Really." She paused. "Did your mother tell you that someone is watching the house?"

"*What?*" He started and glanced around him. "No. Who? Has she seen someone?"

"She's probably keeping it from you so that you won't worry. This person she's consulting is telling her that she's in danger. That…" she swallowed. "That it's a message from your father. That's why she came to me, to see if I could tell her more."

A spark of fury lit Nick's eyes. "A message from my *father*?"

"I'm afraid so. She's going to some medium."

Another beat of silence, and then he finally nodded. "We can't talk here. If Mom comes out to call Rusty in, she'll see the truck. It's kind of distinctive, you know."

Georgie glanced at the maroon canopy designed to tone with her gypsy trailer and had to agree. "Then where?"

"There's a strip mall a few minutes away, with a Starbucks."

Relieved, Georgie nodded. "Get in. Let's go."

Away from his immediate neighborhood, Nick seemed to relax more, and Georgie decided to be assertive right upfront. "I'll tell you what I know, Nick, which isn't much. We'll see if we can pool our knowledge. But first, let me tell you about a couple of other people I've helped." Without using anyone's name, she gave him a quick summary of the con man that Kaylene had narrowly escaped and about James West being framed for industrial espionage.

Nick listened intently, his eyes never leaving her face.

"That's it," she said. "I told you I'd been doing this only a few months, but I've managed to help a couple of people. So far, your mother has paid me twenty dollars a session. She's been to see me three times." She looked down at her latte and played with the spoon. "I don't want to insult you, but I'm guessing that your family can ill afford sixty dollars a week on fortune-telling sessions. Eighty dollars, if you count the twenty that you gave me."

His face tightened, but he nodded.

She cast around for a way to help him save face. "Nick, the charlatans in my field make my blood boil. A lot of what I do *is* for pure entertainment. People come to have a fortune-telling session rather than see a movie or buy a book to read. But sometimes, I meet people in real need of help—like the ones I just told you about." She looked him in the eye. "If I can help people to get justice, to right a few wrongs, I don't need payment. It seems the right way to use what small gift I have." She slid her hand in her pocket and brought out four folded twenty-dollar bills, and held them out to him. "You and your mother fit into that category. It's like pro bono work for a lawyer."

His gaze dropped to the money, and she saw the battle he fought with his pride. Finally, he reached over and took it and then tucked it into a worn brown leather wallet. "We have some bills that need paying."

She watched him put the wallet back into his pocket. "That wallet was your dad's."

He grinned wryly. "Please, don't tell me that he's standing behind me telling you that."

"If he is, I can't see or hear him. But that's an example of what I sometimes pick up," Georgie said quietly. "I *know* that it's his." An image, somewhat hazy, came into her mind. "And somewhere in it, there's a picture of him with your mother, in the snow. They're both wearing red ski jackets."

A muscle in his jaw twitched. "I keep it behind my driver's license." His forehead creased in a frown. "You did that without your crystal ball. Do you really need it?"

With a jolt, Georgie realized he was right. The knowledge about his wallet, the photo…she had picked it up without even thinking about it. She had read about this online. Some people with the Sight could get the same results with cards, or tea leaves, or a crystal ball. Or if they let themselves open up to possibilities, with nothing.

She looked up to find him watching her, his eyes still curious. "I thought I did. Apparently, I don't—not all the time. So, will you help me, Nick?"

He sat back, visibly letting go of some of the strain. "Yes. What do you want me to do?"

Georgie breathed a sigh of relief. Waiting for him in the truck, she'd had time to come up with a brief plan. She could fine-tune it with the others back at the RV park later, but it was a start.

She began to outline her idea.

CHAPTER 7

Lies and Deception

Georgie wasn't sure whether her plan would work, but it was worth a try. She had two main goals for her visit to Katherine, after giving Nick time to pick up his gym things and leave the house again. The first was to probe gently to see if she could find out more about the mysterious medium. The second was to plant a few suggestions about Nick.

Katherine was thrilled to see her, but was evasive when it came to sharing information about the medium she was seeing. "She doesn't see a lot of clients, and she insists on confidentiality," she said. "You know what it's like, I'm sure. You saw how Nick was with you. She gets that kind of thing all the time." She went on with vague details about how the woman had been ridiculed and hounded and now took clients by referral only… and had only agreed to give Katherine extra sessions because a message from 'beyond the veil' warned of danger.

Georgie didn't push. She moved on to the next item, smoothly leading into it by referring to the supposed 'stalker', as Katherine called the person who was allegedly watching her.

"This person watching the house, Katherine," she said. "Has Nick noticed anything?"

Katherine's face closed up. "I haven't told him."

Georgie already knew that, but it served to bring Nick into the conversation. "Forgive me for asking, but was Nick close to his dad?"

"Very, when he was little. He was a good football player himself. Had Nick out there with a football from the time he was old enough to toddle." Katherine's face grew sad at the memory. "I really hope he gets a scholarship."

"He will," Georgie assured her, with complete confidence.

She brightened. "He really will?"

"He really will. His dad would have been proud. It's a pity he couldn't tell him that, isn't it?" Inwardly, Georgie felt bad for saying it, but she couldn't think of any other way to persuade Katherine to take him with her when she next went to see the medium. "Do you think Nick will go along with you one day, and try to make contact himself?"

"B—" Katherine stumbled, catching herself before she gave away a name. "My medium wouldn't allow it. Not after what I've told her about Nick."

"You told her that he's upset about his aunt?"

"His aunt…?" Belatedly, Katherine remembered that her son was supposed to have an aunt. "Um, yes. She knows he hates all psychics. I haven't told her about the trick he pulled with you."

"Did you tell her that you've been to see me?" Georgie asked idly, appearing to focus on the crystal ball.

"No. She's warned me about going to see anyone else. She says there are a lot of frauds out there, and she doesn't want to see me fall victim to them again." She added swiftly, "I'm not including you in that number, of course."

"Again? You mean you've been caught before?"

"Not really, no," Katherine said. "There was one who couldn't tell me much, but I wised up to her pretty quickly."

Georgie was getting nowhere fast here. Katherine would lie as much as she needed to protect this medium of hers.

What was she going to do? Wait around and follow Katherine herself? Get Nick to do it? Get Scott to do it?

If she could only find out who it was, and where she was, she could pose as a client herself.

Come on, she urged the crystal ball. Come on.

Nothing.

This was like being a beginner again, when she hadn't had a single clue about what to expect.

Katherine's hesitant voice brought her back to reality. "Can you tell who it is stalking me?"

"Sorry, no." Georgie sat back, and looked at her watch. "It'll be time for me to head off soon. Didn't you say that Nick usually gets home at around five?"

"Yes. I guess you'd better leave. He's just not prepared to listen to reason about this. But he won't go to the police about you, I promise." Katherine stood, and slid a twenty-dollar bill out from under a vase on a dresser. "Is twenty enough? You've been here for twice as long."

Georgie waved the money away. "It's fine. You get a bulk discount. You don't pay for any more than three readings in one week."

"Really? I've never had that happen before."

Georgie just smiled, and packed up to go. "Katherine?"

Katherine looked at her, still clutching the money.

"Do me a favor? If you're worried about anything, come and see me. I'll be around Santa Monica for another week yet. All included in what you've already paid."

"Thank you. I will."

When Georgie left, Katherine stood at the door gazing after her while she climbed inside the truck, and then waved with a smile as Georgie drove past.

It isn't fair, Georgie thought in anger. *It just isn't fair.*

There was no way this fake self-styled medium was going to get away with it.

CHAPTER 8

Written in the Stars

W hen Georgie drove into the RV park, the first thing she saw was Scott disappearing into his camper. Perfect, just the person she needed to talk to. She parked and made a beeline for his place.

The door was open, and as she approached, she could see him inside, standing at the sink cutting up vegetables.

"Hellooo," she called, heading up the steps.

"C'mon in." He kept chopping, pausing to wave at the dinette as she came through the door. "Take a seat. How'd it go?"

"Not great." Georgie had filled the others in on her plans before she left, so he was pretty much up to speed. "Nick finally seems to believe maybe I'm not a fake after all, but Katherine's staying tight-lipped about this medium of hers." She watched him cut the bushy leaves off baby carrots, leaving just a green tuft on top and put them in a dish. There was a roast in the oven, and the smell made her mouth water and her stomach rumble.

Scott heard and laughed. "Stay for dinner?"

"I was hoping you'd ask." She grinned. "Hope it won't be too long. I'm starving."

"Around an hour. We'll stave off the hunger pangs with a drink and a snack."

Scott sliced a cucumber, arranged the slices on a plate, and added a small tub of cheese dip. Then he poured two glasses of wine. "Here. You sound as though you need this." He put a drink in front of her, along with the dip, and slid into the seat opposite.

She checked out the label of the bottle on the kitchen bench. "My favorite white again. Do you have an endless supply?"

"I bought a few extra bottles when I realized how much you like it."

She nodded and then scooped some of the dip with a slice of cucumber and ate it. Finally, she looked up at him. He was just waiting patiently, his face calm. His lips naturally turned up at the corners, just a little, which lent him an expression of permanent good humor.

"You're so calm," she said. "It's restful."

"So my mother always said."

"Does that mean you were an angelic child?"

He made a face. "Pretty much. My brother gave me a hard time because of it. Made him look bad, even when he was just being a normal kid." He shot her a look. "I didn't try to be the good boy. Just happened that way."

"What's your brother's name?"

"Jeff. But we call him Bluey, most of the time."

"Bluey?"

"He's a redhead."

Georgie shook her head. "I don't get it."

"It's irony."

She pondered that for a moment and then nodded and drank another mouthful of wine. "I'm out of my depth with this Nick thing." It felt good to admit it. Sometimes she felt that being able to read a crystal ball made her think that she should be able to figure out anything. She couldn't.

"And it's eating at you because Nick came to you for help."

"Well, he didn't actually. He came to prove that I was a fraud so that he could have me arrested."

"A minor hiccup."

That earned a smile, but she said: "Don't make me laugh. It's serious. We were right; it was Katherine who lost all the money to some fake psychic online. Nick doesn't have an aunt." She went on to tell him how the afternoon had played out. "If we could just get a name from Katherine, we could do an online search to see if I can get an appointment. If she's a fake, I should be able to spot it. But Katherine's clamming up. Now what?"

Scott had stayed quiet, listening to her and getting up halfway to check the roast and baste it with the pan juices. He looked perfectly at home in the compact kitchen and was a neat cook, rinsing and drying things as he went.

"I'll have to give it thought." He opened a cupboard and pulled out a couple of plates, set into a rack that kept them secure for travel.

"You're the right kind of person to live in a small space," Georgie mused, watching him. "A place for everything and everything in its place. No wonder you look comfortable in my trailer. Jerry always looks as though he wants to punch holes in the walls to make more room."

"He likes his slides, I've noticed." Scott nodded

at the wall of the dinette. "He should approve of this, then."

"What, just one slide in the whole camper?" Georgie mocked. "Not nearly enough."

He topped up their wine and looked at her speculatively. "Okay, so Nick's onside, but Katherine's secretive. You're sure that this medium is conning her?"

"Yes. As certain as I can be, considering that as usual, I don't have any actual *facts*."

He picked up on the frustration in her voice. "It's always going to be that way for you, Georgie. You'll know things that other people can't know, and often you won't be able to prove it. All you can do is keep digging and nudge people to do the right thing. Shine a spotlight on things."

Shine a spotlight on things. Georgie imagined a bright beam of light exposing nasty secrets hidden in dark corners, lighting up the faces of shadowy villains. She liked that idea.

"And if I can't help?"

"Then you can't. You need to be able to live with that." Scott stood up and opened the oven door, and a heavenly smell wafted out. "Let's see if we can come up with a plan after dinner. Time to relax." He set the roasting pan on a heatproof mat and reached up to flick a switch on the overhead cabinet. Soft classical music filled the air.

That sounded just fine to Georgie.

As it turned out, their after-dinner plans didn't include any discussion about exposing fake mediums or the difficulty of bringing people to justice without any actual proof. Instead, they opened a second bottle of wine and caught up on each other's family history. Georgie discovered that Scott had not only a brother called Bluey who did "something with computers", but two sisters, Viv and Lissa, who co-owned a cafe in a country town. His father was a retired long-haul truck driver who could fix or build anything and spent much of his time helping out friends or family.

From the way Scott talked about them, Georgie could tell they were a close family. She envied him that. "I always wanted a sister," she told Scott. "But no, I just have Jerry."

"But thanks to Jerry, you have Tammy," he pointed out. "Just as good as a sister. And you can share my sisters."

Georgie flicked him a glance. Did he mean 'you

can share mine' as a casual comment, or 'you can share mine' as in her future sisters-in-law? What was she supposed to say to that?

Nothing, she decided, reaching for the bottle and tipping the last thimble-full into her glass. When in doubt, say nothing.

Scott grinned at her and wriggled back comfortably in his seat. "Did you know every thought shows on your face?"

"They do not."

"Yes, they do. And just for future reference…." He paused and looked at her, his eyes glimmering with humor. "I'm going to marry you one day. But don't worry about it now."

Georgie choked on her wine, and she felt her heart leap while her eyes met his.

And *blip*, just like that, instead of her worrying about what it all meant and whether it was pre-ordained or whether she'd even like him enough to marry him or how dare he presume, she felt a kind of warm tide flow through her, and something settle into place.

He was right; they would. But it didn't do to let any male get too comfortable. Not even someone as calm and centered as Scott.

"Well," she said, "we'll see."

"That was what my mother always said when she meant 'no'," Scott observed, watching her finish off the tiny amount in the bottom of her glass. "But not you."

"I'm the fortune-teller here," Georgie reminded him, hiding a smile. "I'm not hearing any voices telling me there's a wedding in my future."

"But I'm from a long line of astrologers. It's written in the stars."

Thrown off course, Georgie considered that. "You are? How many generations?"

"Counting me, two."

"Two."

"Yup. Mum, then me." Scott finished off his wine and then took both empty glasses to the sink and rinsed them.

"I haven't seen you do a horoscope ever since I've known you. Or open a pack of cards."

"You don't know what I do in the privacy of my camper. I might do a spread every night." Scott put his hand under her elbow and drew her out of her seat and up into his arms. "I knew you'd be here tonight. Why else do you think I prepared dinner for two?"

"Because you could use the leftovers tomorrow if I didn't turn up?"

"Skeptic." He nodded to the right, where his bed was looking invitingly comfortable. "Stay tonight?"

Georgie rested her head against his chest and smiled, where he couldn't see her and injected doubt in her voice. "Only if it's written in the stars."

"Loud and clear." She felt laughter rumble in his chest. "Tomorrow night too."

"Don't push your luck." Even as she said it, her arms crept around him and hugged him tightly, giving her away completely.

Rosa had seen him in her crystal ball. Scott's mother had seen Georgie in the stars.

It was meant to be, she thought, and put all thoughts of awkward teenage boys and fake mediums out of her mind for a few hours.

CHAPTER 9

A Plan

It was Tammy who finally came up with an idea for finding out who the mystery medium might be.

"I've got to do something while I hang around here waiting to see what Jerry does with the vintage division," she said to Georgie, paying a visit before the day's fortune-telling sessions started. "So why not go undercover?" Her gaze alighted on the pink ceramic pig that sat beside the crystal ball, and she leaned forward to peer at the words printed on the sticky note adhering to its rotund belly: *Donations to Red Cross.* "What's this?"

"My new policy." Georgie beamed with satisfaction. "I'm just doing this for fun from now on. It's donation-only, and it's all going to a good cause."

Tammy pursed her lips. "You're doing readings for free?"

"Yes, and only when I feel like it. It's kind of stage-dressing for the gypsy trailer, but people who need me will find their way somehow."

Tammy thought it through. "You don't need the money because of the commissions for vintage trailers and consults on design… and nobody can call you a fake because the readings are just for fun."

"Exactly. *And* I've got a new line of clothing coming up," Georgie reminded her. "Win-win."

"Is this because of Nick and his mother?"

"Kind of," Georgie admitted, "but I never liked taking money for doing this."

Tammy shook her head. "No wonder Jerry always says you don't have a business head on your shoulders." Then she held up both hands. "I did not just mention Jerry's name. I am not thinking about Jerry."

"Mmm," Georgie said, "so I can see. Now, what's this about going undercover?"

Tammy ran through her reasoning. One, Katherine wasn't likely to give up a name. Two, trying to follow her had its problems. They couldn't sit around outside Katherine's house all day and night waiting for her to go out, not even if they did it in shifts, like real detectives. Three, Nick couldn't follow his mother because he was either at school or football practice or the gym most of the time, and he didn't have a car anyway.

"So I thought," Tammy said, "you could phone her and tell her that you had new information and to come and see you— but then you can be late for the appointment, so she has to wait. I'll be waiting too, and I'll have a story ready to convince her that I need to see a medium."

"There's a slight problem," Georgie said. "I don't have any new information. I've asked the crystal ball."

Tammy waved that off. "Invent something. It's all for the greater good."

"Can't do that. No fake stuff. Never ever." Georgie thought of what her great-grandma Rosa had told her once, about Rosa's own completely talentless mother making up fortunes or winkling the information out of people without their realizing it. Rosa, who really could see the future, was dead against it. So was Georgie. At least that was one thing they agreed on.

Tammy leaned her chin on her hand, furrowing her brow at the pink pig while she thought. "All right, fair enough. Tell her the truth then—that nobody is watching the house, and if there's someone out to get her, it's coming from somewhere else. *That's* true enough, isn't it?"

"She'll be scared out of her mind if I tell her that."

"Then tell her…tell her that you see *good* things coming her way too. Good people who will help her and bring positive things into her life." She raised an eyebrow. "True?"

Georgie gave in. "All right. I'll do it."

She made the call, and an excited Katherine agreed to come that afternoon at two o'clock for the first afternoon reading.

At two that afternoon, Georgie was peeking through the window of Scott's camper, waiting for Katherine to arrive.

Tammy sat slumped at a picnic table near Georgie's trailer with her hair pulled back in a stubby ponytail and dressed in a shapeless cotton sweater over denim shorts. Somehow, she had managed to look downtrodden and almost plain.

"How does she do that?" Georgie marveled.

"She usually has men panting and tripping over their tongues, but today nobody would give her a second glance."

"Talent," said Layla, shoulder to shoulder with her. "Tammy could have been an actress; I've told her often enough. It's in the expression. See how she's got her mouth turned down?"

"And the pose," Georgie said. "She's gone all round-shouldered."

"All in all," Scott put in from where he was relegated to the kitchen table, "a talented member of the CBI team."

Then Georgie let out a gasp of disbelief. "Oh no. You've got to be kidding."

Layla frowned and put her nose against the window. "Is that *Nick*?"

"It's Nick. Something's gone wrong." Georgie kept watching through the window for a few more minutes while Tammy engaged Nick in conversation, and then Tammy looked over towards Scott's camper and waved them across.

"Damn," Georgie muttered. She looked at Layla and went outside, hurrying down the steps with the others behind her.

Nick watched them approach; a deep crease between his eyebrows and his hands fisted in his baggy jacket pockets. He looked entirely too worn down for a kid his age. His eyes moved from Georgie to the others behind her.

Tammy had magically straightened up. She dragged the rubber band off her ponytail and shook out her blonde waves, and then yanked off the threadbare sweater that they'd dug out of the RV park Lost' n' Found box to reveal a form-fitting tank top. Suddenly she was pretty again. Nick blinked, watching the transformation with disbelief.

"Nick says that his mother's not coming," she greeted them.

"What happened?" Georgie searched his face. "Did something give us away?"

Nick sighed. "She told that medium about coming to see you, how you were"—his mouth twisted—"another reputable psychic, and you had news for her. But guess what happened then?"

"She told your mother to stay away from me, I'm assuming, since Katherine's not here."

Nick nodded. "She told Mom she'd had another message from my father. He warned her that she was in danger of falling victim to false prophets... that she was too trusting yet again."

"But I'm not *charging* anything."

"Mom told her that. She said it was a devious

way of gaining her trust and that if you couldn't get to her one way, you'd try it another—through me."

"That's how Nick found out that his mother was supposed to see you today," Tammy said. "Madam Fakery told his mum to make sure Nick didn't go anywhere near you either."

"Mom told her all about how I videoed our session," Nick said, looking despondent. "I was hoping to use my pen on her if I could find out who she was. I can't now. She'll be on to me."

"What a mess." Georgie slid on the seat beside Tammy. "Sit down, Nick. Council of war, everybody. What do we do now?"

Layla sat beside Nick and Scott squeezed in beside Georgie. Seeing Nick's perplexed expression as his gaze moved from one to the other, Georgie explained. "Meet the brains trust, Nick. Crystal Ball Investigations at your service."

He looked slightly dazed. "What?"

"A kind of informal criminal investigation team," Scott said, grinning at him. "We have no evidence and no authority, and a crystal ball that works when it feels like it, but we try hard."

"And you," added Georgie wryly, "have better spy equipment than we do. Actually, we don't have any."

Tammy folded her arms and sighed. "I was really pumped to go undercover, too."

There was a glum silence for a moment, and then Nick spoke up, his words hesitant. "You still can, if you like."

All heads swung his way.

"Don't be offended," he said, his gaze swiftly touching on Tammy's generous curves and jittering away again, color rising in his face. "It's just an idea."

They waited.

"Well, I was thinking, one thing that might make Mom take me along to this psychic…what if I came home with someone totally unsuitable? Like, um," he swallowed, stealing a glance at Tammy again. "Like trailer trash."

Seeing the expression on Tammy's face, Layla let out a crack of delighted laughter. "Tams! That's so *you*!"

Scott was biting back a smile, but Georgie joined Layla, gripping Scott's arm and choking with laughter while Tammy glared at Nick.

Aghast, he inched away from Tammy, close enough to smack him one. "No, no! I didn't mean you *are*, but you could act like it. I mean, look at who you were pretending to be when I arrived, and look at you now. You could be like, undercover trailer trash, and when Mom freaks out, I could say I'll only listen to what Dad says and—oh, jeez."

Finally, Georgie managed to speak. "I think what he's trying to say, Tams, is that you are a good enough actress to pull it off."

Tammy frowned at Nick. "Is that what you meant?"

"Yes," he said miserably. "You know, too much makeup, tight clothes, all that."

"Ah. So I'm to be a trashy cradle snatcher." Tammy's brow cleared as she contemplated her changed role. A speculative glint entered her eye. "Ooh. Yes, I could enjoy that." She reached over and tested Nick's biceps, grinning.

His face now flaming red, he jerked back.

"Right," said Tammy. "Let's work out Plan B."

CHAPTER 10

On the Right Track

Nick, it turned out, had already skipped school to come and see Georgie, but she refused to let him pass on football training as well.

"Training is *important*, Nick," Georgie told him severely. "I can see your *potential* future, but if you keep blowing off training, your coach will dump you, no matter how good you are. No college scholarship then."

Nick flushed. "Yeah, he's already said."

Georgie rolled her eyes. "And yet here you are, all set to miss training again. The future can change, you know. We all make choices at any fork in the road."

"Okay, okay." Some of the old Nick's spirit

returned, and he gave her a sulky look. "No need to nag."

"Right, then off you go." Georgie crossed her arms and gave him the death stare. "You've got my number. Call me when you can talk, and we'll work out a plan."

She watched him slouch off and then turned to find the others all looking at her with varying degrees of amusement. "What?"

"He brings out the mom in you," Layla said, grinning. "You'll be telling him to make his bed next."

"And what's all this about making choices and the future not being set?" asked Tammy. "I've never heard you say that before. I thought it was all, like, "This shall come to pass, watch out!""

"I don't know," Georgie said, nettled. "It just felt right. I'm still learning, all right?"

Scott gave her a light tap on the nose. "You're right, anyway. My mum has warned people in time to change the wrong path in life. She's saved more than one kid from a night in a cell." He nodded at Nick's disappearing back. "The way he's feeling about Katherine's situation, he could do something foolish. He needed a bit of support. *And* nagging."

"Speaking of nagging…" Georgie dug her cell

phone out of a deep pocket in her skirt. "I've meant to phone Rosa for days. She was in on the first meeting with Nick, then nothing." She scrolled through her contacts and stabbed at Rosa's name. "See if I can pin her down to something. It might be time I put her on speed dial as a consultant, with the lack of success I'm having."

She listened at the ringing on the other end for a full minute, then hit 'end'. "I'll give her a few minutes and then try again. If she's out in the garden, it takes her a while to reach the phone."

"No cell phone?" Tammy asked.

"We're lucky she agreed to a landline. As for answering machines—no chance."

The second time, Rosa answered, saying immediately: "Hello, Georgie! How nice to hear from you. Enjoying the sunshine over there in LA?"

Georgie wasn't surprised that Rosa knew who was calling, despite the lack of caller ID on her old-fashioned phone. Rosa always knew. "Yes, thanks. We're in a park in Santa Monica." Georgie pressed the speaker button so the others could hear. "How's your arthritis?"

"Just fine," Rosa said crisply, "but I'm sure you didn't call me to talk about that. What's up with your phone? You sound like you're talking underwater."

"I've got you on speaker so the others can hear, but I can take it off if it's annoying."

"No, keep going. Your Leo is there, isn't he? And two others."

Layla's eyes widened, but Tammy just grinned. She had met Rosa enough times to know what she could do. "Hi, Mrs. Goode. It's Tammy here."

"I told you before, make it Grandma Rosa or Great Gran, like everybody else." There was a familiar bark of laughter at the other end. "You've got that young pup Jerry running around not knowing which way to jump. I knew you'd be good for him."

"Good," Tammy said, her eyes narrowing. "He's got some fences to mend. Has he moved vintage trailers behind the shed yet?"

"Lots of talk, not much action. Want my advice? Keep him off balance for a while yet. I'm enjoying this."

Tammy brightened. "Don't worry; I will."

"You're calling about young Nick," Rosa went on. "I see all of you involved in this. Be careful."

"We're all involved in it because I'm not getting anything from the crystal ball," Georgie broke in, seizing her chance. "You were there on the first day Nick came, but after that… nothing. Nothing from you, and nothing from the crystal ball. Am I doing something wrong?"

"Nope," Rosa said cheerfully. "When it's time for you to know, it'll tell you."

Georgie frowned at the phone, frustrated. "Then why did you tell me about his dog the first time? Why is this important enough for you to turn up at all?"

"Who said it has to be important for me to show up?" Rosa countered. "I like to pop in now and then just to see what's going on. I'm an old woman; there's not much in my life now."

Georgie could picture her sitting there, her lips stretched in the familiar wide gummy grin, her black eyes sparkling with humor. An image appeared in her mind, momentarily as clear as a reflection in a still pool before it flickered out. Rosa wasn't sitting; she was standing, staring out of the window at the neighbor's big tabby, washing itself in the sun. Over the fence, Georgie had caught a hint of movement: the man next door pushing a mower around.

She crossed her fingers and gave in to impulse, hoping she was right. "I don't know," she said. "You can always watch the cat next door. Or Bobby Carston mowing. There's always something going on in your neighborhood."

There was a brief silence, and then Rosa said sincerely, "Good girl, Georgie. I always knew. Always."

The sense of relief Georgie felt was out of proportion to the glimpse of Rosa's life. She *could* do it. She could.

The others looked from Georgie to the cell phone as though they were trying to see what she could see at the other end of the conversation. She smiled at them weakly and tried again.

"Please, Rosa. Just tell me, am I missing something? This fortune-telling stuff fades in and out like bad TV. Meanwhile, Nick needs help. Him and his mother."

Rosa heaved a sigh that rattled through the speaker. "Have some faith in yourself, girl. Life's not all about what comes to you through the crystal ball —or tea leaves, or scrying bowls, or the cards that your young Leo likes to consult."

They all looked at Scott, and he just shrugged and opened his hands in a 'she got me' gesture.

"You've got brains, and you've got friends. And young Nick needs to be part of this, not just have you find out from a crystal ball. If he helps to fix this, his mother will listen to him next time."

"So we're on the right track?"

"Didn't I just tell you to have faith in yourself? And your friends? That's enough talk, now. I've got a cat to watch."

With that, Rosa was gone.

Georgie looked around at the others. "Was that a vote of confidence in Crystal Ball Investigations that I just heard?"

"Definitely," Tammy said. "Looks like I'd better go and dig out a trailer trash outfit." She pushed herself up from the table and grinned. "So, Jerry doesn't know which end is up, hey? Another win."

She sauntered off.

Layla cocked her head on one side and stared at Scott. "I get the reference to 'young Leo', but what's this about consulting the cards? You been holding out on us?"

"Not at all," Scott said. "But I just do it for entertainment." He winked at Georgie. "Don't want to steal your thunder."

A thought occurred to Georgie. "You haven't picked up anything about Nick's case, have you?"

"Of course not. Otherwise, I would have told

you all at the team briefing. Nope, it's as much of a mystery to me as it is to you."

All right, thought Georgie, mulling over both Scott's words and the conversation with Rosa. Perhaps this is what's written in the cards. They were meant to solve this as a team, including the newest member: a sometimes-sulky but well-meaning teenager.

Life was never dull.

CHAPTER 11

Trailer Trash

Tammy couldn't remember the last time she'd had this much fun. Part of it was watching Nick try to keep his eyes off her various assets, displayed to advantage in a push-up bra, midriff top, and low-slung steel-gray capris made of some evil fabric that didn't breathe and felt slimy to the touch. She'd unearthed those from the lost-and-found box too. Funny how all the clothes in the box were those that nobody would ever want to be returned.

She activated the phone mirror app and checked her makeup. Too much eye shadow, too much lipstick, too much thick foundation, and artfully applied dark roots to her messed-up blonde hair. Although it had pained her to do something so nasty to her Marilyn Monroe waves, she particularly liked that touch.

"Perfect," she said to Nick, slipping the phone into her shiny turquoise vinyl handbag and beaming at him. "Ready to go?"

They were in Scott's truck because it was much less recognizable than Georgie's. Scott and Georgie had both swiveled around from the front seat for a last-minute briefing.

Georgie looked at Nick's video pen in his pocket. "Are you sure she won't know you're recording this?"

"I don't think so. Even if she does, I've got my voice-activated digital recorder here too." He patted his pants pocket.

"Wow," Tammy said in admiration. "The well-equipped spy."

Nick blushed. "It's not really for spying. I use it in class." He looked back at his house, just down the road, looking nervous.

Tammy squeezed his arm. "C'mon Nick; it'll be fine. This was your idea, remember?"

"I know. Mom's going to be so mad, though." Another long moment went by, and then he huffed out a quick breath and opened the door. "Let's get it over with."

Tammy opened her door and slid out. She bent down at Georgie's window and winked. "Showtime. I always wanted to do this."

Georgie widened her eyes at her innocently. "Be trailer trash?"

"Be an undercover detective." Tammy shifted some gum around in her mouth, straightened up, and hitched her bag over her shoulder. "See you later."

She hurried after Nick, her gold flip-flops slapping the road as they crossed to his house.

"Are you sure she's in?" Tammy said to his back.

"She usually is." Looking apprehensive, Nick tried the door, which opened right away. "She's here."

"Try not to look as though you're going to an execution," Tammy whispered in his ear. "You're smitten with me, remember?"

Nick gave a sick smile and led the way along the small hallway into the kitchen, calling: "Mom?"

"Here, sweetie," came Katherine's cheerful voice from the adjacent open-plan living room. "How was training?"

"Good. Er, mom…"

He stopped, and Tammy peered around him. Katherine was comfortably ensconced on the sofa, reading. She glanced up and then did a double-take, swinging her legs onto the floor. "Oh. Um, hi! Nick, who's this?"

Her voice was still polite, but the expression in her eyes changed as Nick moved aside to let Tammy past.

"Hiya, Mrs…uh…" Tammy stopped and cheerfully punched Nick on the arm. "Nicky, you never told me your last name!"

"Ahern," he mumbled.

"Mrs. Ahern." Tammy grinned at her cheerfully. "Nice place you got here. Bit more room than in my trailer."

"Nick," said Katherine, closing a book entitled *Messages from Beyond* and setting it carefully down on the coffee table, "I thought you were supposed to be at football training?"

"I was," Nick said quickly. "You know Coach Mason said miss once more, and I was out, so I went. Tammy and I had coffee after."

"Ah." Katherine's gaze grew colder. "And where did you meet Tammy? At school?"

Tammy let out a screech of laughter. "School? I haven't been to school for years. I do haircuts at the RV park. Not trained or nuthin', I just have the knack." She reached up to ruffle Nick's hair.

"Nicky's probably just about due for a cut. I could do wonders with it." She eyed Katherine's nondescript greying hair. "I can do yours too if you like. Put some color in it, give it a lift."

Katherine's eyes flicked to Tammy's dark roots and her lips twisted in an involuntary grimace. "No, thank you."

Tammy moved closer to Nick and poked him meaningfully in the back. His performance so far wasn't winning any Oscars.

"Sit down, Tammy," he said, galvanized. "Would you like a soda?"

"Soda?" She grimaced. "Have you got a beer?"

"Nicky isn't old enough to drink," Katherine snapped. "Although you seem to be."

"Yep," said Tammy cheerfully, plunking herself down next to Katherine. "I passed the big 2-1 a couple of years ago now. Mind you; I never used to let being underage stop me." She winked at Nick. "Bet you don't either, Nicky. You wouldn't be a football player if you didn't sneak a beer on the quiet now and then. And we all know about football parties."

"*Do* we?" Katherine's voice was pure ice. "Have you been holding out on me, Nick?"

"No," he said quickly and then changed his

tune when he saw Tammy widening her eyes at him meaningfully. "Well, only a little bit."

"A little bit?"

"C'mon, Mom. Dad used to tell me about the parties you went to," Nick said defensively.

"He did *not*."

"Well, not in detail, but he said you used to have some wild parties. Well, now it's my turn." He stuck out his bottom lip mutinously, hitched himself on the arm of the settee next to Tammy, and slung his arm around her neck.

Better, thought Tammy. Now he was getting into character. She reached up and linked her fingers with his, tugging his hand down dangerously close to the push-up bra, and sent him a fond look. "Don't you worry, Mrs. Ahern. Nicky's all right. You should see some of the guys I've been out with in the past. Made my dad's hair curl. He's glad I've found a nice boy at last."

"Nick is still at *school*," Katherine said in a choked voice. "He's got football and college to think about. And I think he's a bit young for you."

"There are only five years between us," Tammy said, sounding aggrieved. "You think he's too good for me, is that it? Just because I live in a trailer park? Our trailer is neat, you know." Then she amended it. "Well, my mum's trailer is neat. Mine, not so much, now I've got my own. But it's not dirty, just messy. Not that Nicky cares about the mess."

"It's not that bad," Nick contributed. "Why don't you come out to the RV park and meet Tammy's family, Mom? They're nice people. Her mom looks just like Tammy; you'd think they were sisters."

Tammy chewed hard on the wad of gum in her mouth so she wouldn't laugh. Poor Katherine.

She wriggled a bit on the settee and tugged at her stretch capris in a vain attempt to get the wrinkles out where they were riding up on her thigh. Eww, the fabric felt horrible to touch; she'd never encountered anything like it. Feeling Katherine draw away from her, she leaned closer and said in a confidential tone, "These pants are like, so comfortable that I might as well be wearing nothing, but they don't hold their shape. You have that problem with any of your pants, Katherine?"

"Never," said Katherine, averting her eyes from the red lace of Tammy's thong visible just above the hipline of her pants. "Nick, we should give our guest some refreshments. Give me a hand in the kitchen?"

"Jeez, Mrs. Ahern, I'm not a *guest*," Tammy said with a laugh. "I'll help."

"No, no. You just sit here and, um, read this." Katherine grabbed the book from the coffee table and shoved it at her. "We'll be right back."

Tammy watched them go, Nick trailing after his mother's rigid back. She glanced down at the book and flipped through it while listening intently to the hushed, angry tones coming from the kitchen. She caught a few words here and there: pretty much what she expected: too young, and *that woman*, and something about school and football.

Then Nick, low and furious: *"…see who I want to see… Dad would have…"* and more that she couldn't quite catch.

The book seemed to be a collection of stories about communications from dead loved ones. For a moment, Tammy felt a pang of sympathy for Katherine. It sounded as though Nick's dad had been important to both of them. No wonder Katherine was desperate to hold on to whatever she could.

She fanned the pages back to the table of contents, and there it was, on the blank facing page, in a spiky black script: *"To Katherine. Be Guided by the Wisdom from Those who Have Crossed Over. Bianca."*

Bianca. Tammy stared at the name and then closed the book and turned to the back cover.

There was a picture of a middle-aged woman, softly backlit, her face half in shadow. Very mysterious.

Underneath it was a brief bio about the author: Bianca Bellamy.

Swiftly, she skimmed through it. Years of helping others, blah blah blah, select few clients, blah blah…she hunted for a website address or any kind of address, looking at the front matter or the afterword, but there was nothing.

Bianca Bellamy. Hearing that Nick and his mother were still hissing at each other, she dug into her bag for her phone and photographed the bio and the handwritten message. When she heard footsteps, she hastily flipped back to one of the stories and pretended to read.

Katherine's face was tight and closed. Nick's was mutinous.

"Come on, Tammy, we're leaving," he said. "You were right: my mother doesn't think you're good enough for her son."

"But…" Tammy put the book down and let her eyes fill with crocodile tears. "Nicky, that's not fair."

"I know. Come on. We're out of here."

He jerked his head towards the door and strode off, leaving Tammy to follow him.

She walked past his mother and hissed, "Selfish cow. Bet his *Dad* would have liked me!" and left, feeling excruciatingly guilty.

When all this was over, she would apologize to poor Katherine.

CHAPTER 12

Following Clues

Georgie and Scott watched Nick storm out of the house, heading off around the nearest corner, with Tammy flip-flopping along behind him.

"Guess that's our cue," Georgie said. She looked at her watch. "They weren't even in there for ten minutes."

"Looks like Momma Bear didn't take to Tams." Scott started the engine, drove around the corner, and stopped to pick up the two waiting for them.

Tammy hopped in and groaned. "I feel so *guilty*. Poor Katherine. I would have hated me too."

"This had better work," Nick said as he got in from the other side. "She won't be speaking to me for, like, about ten years."

"It was your idea," Tammy reminded him yet again. "Did you ask about the medium?"

"No." Nick sounded impatient. "That would have seemed a bit suspicious, don't you think? I just said *Dad* would have liked Tammy, and *Dad* wouldn't have treated her like something on the sole of his shoe, and I wished that *Dad* was still here. If that isn't enough to send her back to Madame Whatsername, I don't know what is." He put his forearm over his eyes. "I feel like crap."

"Me too, if that's any comfort," said Tammy. "And Madame Whatshername is called Bianca Bellamy."

Nick put his arm down and stared at her.

Georgie turned around as far as she could in the front seat. "You're kidding."

Tammy shrugged. "What can I say? I'm an ace detective."

"What, did she have a phone list on the wall with her down under 'My Favorite Medium'?"

"No phone list," Nick said. "She wouldn't leave a name out anywhere I could see it."

"Oh ye of little faith," Tammy said, then relented. "She was in such a hurry to get Nick out of the room to scream at him about me that she shoved a book at me to keep me occupied. *Voices from Beyond*, something like that."

"*Messages from Beyond*," Nick corrected her. "She must have read it fifty times."

Tammy pulled her phone out of her bag with the air of a conjurer and navigated to photos. "Ta-da!" She turned it around so they could see.

Georgie took the phone from her, and as her eyes met those of the woman on the photographed book jacket, a shiver went through her. It was as though she was staring straight through the photo, right into the depths of the woman's soul. *Pitiless*, she thought. *Avaricious*. Cold crept through her.

Scott's hand closed over her shoulder, and when she looked at him, she could see he knew. "It's her."

"It's her." Avoiding the eyes of the woman in the photo, she swiped to enlarge the text and skimmed the bio, then looked at Tammy again. "*I* know it's her, but how did *you* know? Katherine could have had a dozen books by various mediums and psychics."

"She does," Nick said.

Tammy waved a hand. "Flick to the next photo."

Georgie did so and read the handwritten signed

note from the author. "I see. So you knew she'd met the author."

"As I said—ace detective. Can I have a raise?"

Nick held out his hand, and Georgie handed him the phone. He studied it silently for a moment, flicking back and forth between the photo and the note to his mother in the front.

"I'll have a look in the book when she's not around," he said finally. "See if I can see a website address or something."

"Already did that." Tammy took her phone back. "There were no contact details at all. I don't suppose you can remember how your mother got this book? A bookstore? Online? From a visit?"

Surprisingly, Nick remembered it clearly. "She came home with it, the day she went to see her for the first time…all happy because she'd been given a book as a token of faith. Why didn't I guess that this psychic might have been the author?"

"No wonder she told her that my not charging for visits was a lead-in to a scam," Georgie said. "She probably does it all the time. She'd know all the tricks."

By now, Nick had his phone out, searching Bianca Bellamy. "400,000 hits," he said absently. He tapped some more. "I'll add 'medium'."

"Add 'scam' and 'fake'," suggested Georgie. "If anyone's posted about her, it'll come up. Try the name of the book, too."

Nick hammered away at his phone for a bit, clicked through to a few links, and finally shook his head. "Nothing. Not that I can find quickly."

"Hmm." Georgie was surprised. "You'd think that somebody would have mentioned her. Unless, of course, she uses different names."

"That book could be just for show," Scott contributed. "She could just have a dozen or so printed at a time and be ready to hand them out to any likely targets."

They all sat for a moment, with nobody coming up with anything useful. Now they had a name and a photo that might or might not be real, but no trail.

"We still need an address, or a phone number… anything." Then Georgie had a sudden flicker of memory: Rosa saying, *"Nick needs to be a part of this. He needs to be the one to fix it…"*

"Back to you, Nick," she said firmly. "I can guarantee she's the one. Now you have to either persuade your mother to take you to see her or get a phone number or *something*."

"A signed confession would be good," suggested Tammy.

Scott put in: "Ask your Mom how she first heard about Bianca. That might give us a lead."

"Okay." He opened the door. "I'll go back and tell her that she's insulted Tammy so badly that she isn't speaking to me." A tired grin crossed his face. "Maybe hint that I might need to skip school tomorrow to try to win her back."

"Love your work, Nick." Tammy leaned over to blow him a kiss, which gave him a birds-eye view of generous tanned curves displayed in a handkerchief-sized top, which made him turn bright red again before he stumbled backward and hastened off around the corner.

"Tams," Georgie said reprovingly. "He's just a boy. Have pity on him."

"Big boy, though," Tammy said dreamily. "Imagine him in a few years. College quarterback. All muscle and no pimples."

As she spoke, her phone gave the blip that presaged an incoming video call.

She looked at the display, said "Huh," rolled the gum around in her mouth a few times, and tapped the screen, holding up one finger to signal to Scott and Georgie to hold everything. "Hiya, honey. How ya doin'?"

There was a shocked silence, and then Jerry's voice said, "What in God's name have you done to your hair?"

"It's my new trailer trash look," Tammy said. "Look." She held the phone out and tilted it here and there so Jerry could take in her bare flesh and skin-tight capris, finishing with her gold flip flops. "You like?"

"What the hell are you doing?"

Tammy frowned at the phone while Georgie put a hand over her mouth to hold back the mirth.

"Jerry, that's not very friendly," said Tammy reprovingly.

"You'll be the death of me, Tams. What if someone saw you like that?"

"Well, that's the general idea. I'd hardly dress like this just for me."

Georgie heard an irritated grunt on the other end of the phone and gave Tammy a thumbs up.

"Yes, well." Jerry finally got his voice back, along with an aggrieved note. "I don't know what you're up to, but I've got a nice surprise for you. Not that you deserve it."

Tammy narrowed her eyes at the phone, a move

that made her heavily made-up eyes take on the look of a predatory jungle cat. "Careful, Jer."

"Whatever. Just look at this." There was silence while Tammy stared at whatever Jerry was showing her on his phone. At one point, she glanced up at Georgie, her rosebud lips pressed together in a way that didn't bode well for Jerry B. Goode, and then returned her gaze to the phone.

"Well?" Jerry's voice finally sounded again. "Isn't that just what you had in mind? I found your notes and got exactly what you wanted. Right down to the Chevy ice cream bar!"

There was another silence while Tammy just stared at the screen, and Georgie chewed her fingernails. She had a fair idea of what was going on.

"Tams? Don't just stare at me like that. Tell me what you think?"

"I think," said Tammy, "that I could see the back of the work shed while you were panning around. And, if I wasn't mistaken, the corner of the fence."

"Tams. C'mon. It had to happen. You can't have everything your way. When are you girls going to see reason?"

"Can you do the walk around once more?"

"Sure, babe, sure."

Tammy silently handed the phone to Georgie, who tilted it so Scott could see. The camera panned around to show a row of vintage trailers, all set up with cute outdoor settings, different colors, and styles. Three gypsy trailers were clustered together, with gaily colored shawls flung over a couple of chairs outside.

Just as Tammy had suggested, it was all enclosed inside a charming picket fence. And it was all squeezed into the corner behind the main work shed, a fact that Jerry tried to hide by hastily panning back when it appeared.

Georgie's eyes met Tammy's as she handed back the phone.

War, they promised each other wordlessly.

"See?" came Jerry's voice again. "Your retro lot will love it. I tried hard here, Tams."

"Yes," she said. "I can see that you implemented my ideas faithfully."

Jerry picked up on her meaning right away. "I'm not taking the credit for it. Everyone knows it's all your idea."

"Except for the position."

Jerry gave up and tried another tack. "When are you coming back? I miss you."

"Do you?" Tammy blew a massive bubble of gum, which promptly burst and flattened out over her mouth.

"That's gross, Tam."

"Yeah, but I'm trailer trash now. And I'm not coming back."

"What do you mean you're not coming back?"

"I mean I AM NOT COMING BACK." Tammy's eyes took on a feral gleam. "Not until I'm ready to start my own vintage and retro yard. *Tammy's Traditional Trailers.* Has a ring about it, don't you think?" She turned her phone around so that Jerry was looking straight at the face of his furious sister. "What do you think, Georgie?"

"Sounds good to me," Georgie said to Jerry. "Guess you'd better tell Dad." With that parting salvo, she sat back, and Tammy hit END to cut off his spluttering pleas and threats.

She sat for a moment staring out of the window and then looked back at Georgie. "I knew he'd do it. Dammit." She picked at her ugly stretch pants and heaved a sigh. "Let's go. I've got to get these things off before they stick permanently to my skin."

Quietly, Scott started the engine. Nobody said anything all the way back to the RV park.

CHAPTER 13

Pursuit

The entire next day passed without a word from Nick, and Tammy spent most of the time in her beloved cherry red and white retro trailer looking up startup business grants and crunching numbers, while the furrow between her eyes grew deeper and deeper.

"She's devastated," Georgie said to Layla on the way back from a much-quieter-than-usual morning tea at Tammy's. "Furious with him and so sad. I don't know what to say to her."

"That's because you've lived with Jerry-the-snake your whole life, and you didn't expect anything else. Tams fell in love with him."

"Dammit."

"Yeah. Are you two really going to start up your own vintage trailer yard?"

"To tell you the truth." Georgie said, "I don't want to. I was perfectly happy as part of the road team. Jerry and Tammy were doing great back there until he decided to pull rank. What an idiot."

Layla cast her a sideways look. "Any chance of him changing his mind?"

"He never has before, unless Dad pulls rank on *him*. But if Dad thinks it's for the best, he'll let Jerry have his way. And he *will* think it's for the best because Jerry will talk about nothing but the benefits of the Platinum Customer Care program, which Dad has wanted for years." Georgie flapped a hand. "Don't talk about him."

"Fine," said Layla. "Let's go get Mags and talk about the next Retro rally instead."

Which they cheerfully did, even managing to drag Tammy across for a happy hour drink as the sun went down.

Nobody had heard anything from Nick. They heard nothing the next day either, and by breakfast the third day were surmising that maybe Katherine had locked Nick in a cupboard under the stairs like Harry Potter when he finally phoned.

"At last," said Georgie. "We'd just about given

you up. Wondered if maybe Madame Bianca had banished you to the Other Side."

"School, football, Mom watching me like a hawk," Nick said briefly. "She even went to see the coach to talk about me. I got the fatherly talk about not throwing my life away and how hormones can make teenage boys crazy."

"From what I remember of teenage boys, he's not too far wrong," said Georgie. "So you agreed to stay away from trailer trash?"

"Only if I could get the chance to hear from Dad myself… well, through the medium. Mom wouldn't agree at first, but I wore her down."

Georgie, remembering her brother Jerry working on her mother, could well believe it.

"On the condition that I leave my video pen at home," Nick went on, "and any recording devices. She made me promise. Not that we got anything useful the other day."

"So, where does this person hang out?"

"I don't know. Mom won't say. She says she still doesn't trust me not to do something stupid, so I told her if she felt like that, I'd even agree to be blindfolded while she drives there—and she said OK! Can you believe it? What does she think this is, the Mafia?"

"So says the boy with the video spy pen," Georgie said dryly. "It doesn't matter. We'll follow you."

"Watch that she doesn't see you. It would be better if we could use a tracking device."

"Sadly, I'm right out of those."

There was a heavy sigh from Nick's end. "I was going to order one. I should have."

Georgie shook her head. She liked Nick, but she thought he should stick to football and cheerleaders instead of playing spies.

"Did you find out how your mom first heard of Bianca?"

"Yeah, it was in a chat room. She met her on a forum and then went to a chat room for a consult, and then they met up offline. It sounds like it all took a few months. I'll text you the forum details."

It didn't sound like anything they could use right away, but at least he was trying. "Thanks. So, what time is this happening?"

"It's…hang on." There was a brief silence, then "Mom just came in; gotta go. We go to see her tomorrow when I get home from football training." Abruptly, Nick ended the call.

Georgie looked at the others, who had been listening in avidly. "Hear that? Tomorrow it is."

"I was thinking," said Scott, "maybe we should use two cars. In case one gets caught at traffic lights or something. One could stay ahead of them, one behind." He cast a glance at Georgie's distinctive truck. "Better use mine and Layla's. If you're going to make a habit of stakeouts, you need to buy a truck that blends in."

"No chance." Georgie glanced from the glowing maroon woodwork of her trailer to the matching truck canopy and smiled. A girl had to have a bit of style.

"I can tell your heart's not in this investigation lark," Scott said. "Not when it comes to the practical details."

They tossed around ideas and suggestions for a while and then hung around the forum and a couple of associated chat rooms, but nobody who looked or sounded like Bianca showed up.

"If I had months," Georgie said to Scott, closing her computer far too close to midnight, "I could probably find her. But that'll give her too much time to get her claws into Katherine. We have to move now."

"We do," he agreed. "Have faith. Tomorrow is the day."

As soon as Katherine's ancient Toyota backed out of the driveway the next afternoon, Scott, a hundred yards down the road, started his engine. "Here we go."

"Some investigators we are," Georgie said, feeling tense. "No plan. No clues. We're just following a teenage kid with a blindfold and a woman who spends all her grocery money on psychics. What's wrong with this picture?"

"Roll with it." Calmly, Scott settled in at a cautious distance and followed. He glanced into the rear vision mirror and then reached for the CB. "You there, Layla?"

"Yeah, copy."

"I'm going to go past soon. You stay behind them for a while, and then we'll swap. Let me know if they turn off once I'm past."

"Copy that."

"Wow," said Georgie. She reached across and keyed the mike to talk to Layla. "Listen to us sounding all official. Can't we throw in a few Alpha Delta Tangos?"

Tammy's voice came across the airwaves. "I liked it better when I was playing trailer trash."

A gravelly masculine voice cut in. "Don't mind a bit of trailer trash myself, little girl. Wanna meet up?"

"I beg your pardon," Tammy shot back. "I wasn't talking to you."

"It's not talkin' I had in mind, darlin'."

Scott laughed.

"Hell." Georgie scrabbled for her cell phone and called Tammy. "It's me. Change to a different channel."

"Won't make any difference if they're scanning," Scott observed. "Just use your phone on speaker."

"Did you hear that, Tams?" Georgie asked, tapping the speaker button on her phone.

"Yes," came Tammy's disgusted voice. "I bet the cops don't have this kind of trouble."

"Leave your phone on," Scott advised. "Going past her now, Tams."

He pulled into the next lane and drove past Katherine, looking straight ahead with his ball cap pulled low and sunglasses shading his eyes. Georgie, similarly disguised, turned her head away from the other car.

They drove for about fifteen minutes. For amateurs, Georgie thought, they weren't doing too

badly. As far as she could judge, they were somewhere in West LA when Katherine finally pulled
over to the side of the road, reversing her car to
tuck it in between two others.

Scott was ahead of her but keeping watch in his
rear vision mirror. "That's it," he said. "She's
stopped." He cruised along, hunting for a parking
space, and raised his voice. "You watching, Layla?"

"We're a couple of hundred yards behind,"
came Tammy's voice. "When they get out, we'll
cruise past to see which house she goes in."

"OK."

With a bit of to-ing and fro-ing, both cars finally
managed to park within a block of Katherine's.
Tammy called in to report the house number, and
then they all settled in to wait, with a few desultory
conversations on cell phones.

Finally, Scott nodded at the brightly woven bag
between Georgie's feet. "Go on, have a look. You
won't settle until you do."

She darted a quick look at him. "How did you
know I brought it?"

"I know you. Nick has located her; now see if
you can find out more."

Georgie reached down and pulled the bag onto
her lap. "I just thought...if we could get close to

her, it might somehow trigger something in this…"
She pulled out Rosa's crystal ball, protected by the decades-old black velvet cloth, and unwrapped it.

She had barely laid her hands on it when the white mist appeared.

CHAPTER 14

Confrontation

Georgie drew in an involuntary breath and stared intently at the crystal ball. An image of Bianca flashed into her mind. It was the same woman that Tammy had photographed on the back of the book jacket, but the face seemed sharper, more predatory. The flickering light from a candle in front of the woman's face emphasized her cheekbones.

Georgie closed her eyes and concentrated on the image in her mind.

The psychic's eyes were, at first, focused on the candle, but then she glanced up. Her eyes darted back and forth as though looking from one face to another. Nick and his mother, perhaps?

The image faded. Frustrated, Georgie opened her eyes again and peered at the mist in the crystal ball. Impressions started flooding into her mind— she had no words for what she felt. It was a kind of inner knowing: she sensed corruption and lies, coldness and avarice.

She also felt that Katherine and Nick were entirely out of their depth.

She hastily wrapped the ball again and shoved it into the bag, and let herself out of the car. "She's conning them, I know it. I've got to get in there." On impulse, she opened the door again and picked up the bag.

Scott, as always, was calm. "Want backup?"

"No, but I'll leave my phone on so you can listen." She tapped in his number and then set off.

The whitewashed house that Tammy had flagged was half a dozen houses down the street, but as it turned out, Georgie would have known where to turn in anyway; it was like being pulled by an invisible rope. She opened the gate and walked straight past the house, following the driveway around to a garage that looked like it had been converted into a small apartment.

There was a midnight blue wooden plaque on

the door, with *Bianca* painted on it in silver, in a flowery cursive script.

Georgie didn't bother knocking. She opened the door, and three people sitting around a small round table looked up, startled at the sudden incursion of bright daylight.

"Hi," she said, closing the door behind her so the room returned to its previous ambiance: dim, with all the light coming from one pure white candle on the table. "Sorry to interrupt, but I was… uh…called here." Well, that wasn't telling a lie.

"Excuse me." Bianca had risen halfway to her feet when the door opened, and now she stood fully upright, frowning. "This is a private session—and I don't take anyone without an appointment anyway." Her voice was low and restrained, but Georgie could sense the annoyance behind it. "Who are you? How did you find this place?"

Katherine finally found her voice. "Georgie? What are you doing here?"

Bianca's head whipped around to Katherine. "You know this person?"

"I told you about her. You know…?" Katherine widened her eyes significantly and tapped her forehead.

"I'd be the one you warned Katherine about, I

believe," Georgie said helpfully. "You know, the one who is after her money."

Katherine immediately turned her attention to Nick, looking betrayed. "You told her!"

"Yes." Nick squirmed. "But, Georgie, wait. I'm not sure now…Bianca had a message for us from Dad…" He looked embarrassed…and hopeful.

"Something that she couldn't have known," Katherine said, folding her arms. "We didn't tell her."

Damn Bianca, Georgie thought, furious. She'd read enough about how people like Bianca worked: she would have winkled information about Katherine, fragment by fragment, over the months in a chat room, until Katherine would forget what she'd told Bianca and what she hadn't. And now she was sucking in poor Nick, who was as big a skeptic as any she'd met. She thought fast.

"Bianca, I'm sorry for gatecrashing like this. But—"

But Katherine hadn't finished. "You followed us here, didn't you?" A thought struck her, and she looked accusingly at Nick. "You told her we were coming!"

"I waited outside your house," Georgie said

swiftly, protecting him. "I thought you'd probably go while Nick was at school, but you didn't."

"There are laws about following people," said Katherine huffily.

There weren't, as far as Georgie knew, but she let it go. "I'm sorry. I need to consult Bianca about something I saw in the crystal ball."

"Whatever it is, this is not an appropriate time." Bianca moved towards the door. "Please leave."

Georgie stalled. "Just let me show you this one thing, and I will. It's something that Katherine would want to know."

"No. Out."

As she had hoped, Katherine couldn't resist her last statement. "Wait." She held up a hand. "How could it hurt, Bianca? Just a few minutes. Then we can continue where we left off."

Bianca wavered. Suspicion and anger came off her in waves, but she was skilled in not letting her face show what she thought. She was clearly teetering on the edge between tossing this interloper out and playing the part of the innocent-and-maligned psychic.

"Please." Georgie sent her an imploring look. "Just a few minutes, and I'll go. You'll want to hear this too." She glanced at Katherine again and took a tiny step backward. "But if you truly want me to go…"

Doing a credible job of hiding her anger, Bianca sat down again. "I just hope your presence hasn't blocked the channel. Two minutes. Sit." She gestured at a spare chair over in a corner.

"Thank you." Georgie fetched it, sat, and withdrew her crystal ball, sensing Bianca's curiosity underlying her annoyance. *She probably wants to see how another fraud does it*, thought Georgie.

She set her hands on the crystal ball, focusing on Bianca. *Come on… anything about Bianca.*

As it had in the car, the crystal sphere quickly filled with tendrils of mist, which gradually grew thicker. Katherine and Nick leaned forward, their concentration palpable.

Yet again, Georgie didn't see any pictures or forms in the mist. Instead, the movements of the curling wisps of white seemed to prompt images in her mind, with random words and phrases.

She saw a parade of women, flickering in and out, and names. Some names she saw as though written by hand; some were whispers in her mind.

Nerida… Elizabeth… Shirley. Nerida again.

Elizabeth ELIZABETH ELIZABETH…

A woman's face flashed into her mind; curly red hair; carrying a small black dog.

"What exactly are you supposed to be showing us?" Bianca asked, sounding bored. "I do not see anything."

"Me either," said Katherine. She glanced up at Georgie. "Georgie…?"

Suddenly, Georgie got a place: *Reno*. The name image was accompanied by the rear view of a brick house shaded by palm trees, showing a pool sparkling in the sun and a figure coming through the back door. Bianca; she *knew* it was Bianca, although the hair color was different. The image flashed in and out of Georgie's mind so quickly she barely had time to assimilate it.

"This is going nowhere," Bianca said with a tone of finality. "I think we're done."

The candle flame, flickering on her face, made her look faintly threatening in the dim room.

Go with it, Georgie told herself. This was how it worked for her…get started, and the words would flow, faster and faster.

"Before here," she said, "you lived in a house in Reno. Blonde brick, with a pool."

Opposite her, Bianca froze. "I never lived in Reno."

Undeterred, Georgie went on. "You left because of…Elizabeth." That name wouldn't go away. "Yes, Elizabeth. A woman with red hair. She owned a little black dog."

"You're wasting my time. I don't know any Elizabeth, with or without a dog."

"What about Shirley? Or Nerida?" Georgie looked up, now sure of her ground. "If I started searching, Bianca, what would I find?"

Images tumbled through her mind: Bianca and a parade of people, *money money money…* and again, *Elizabeth*. "What happened to Elizabeth? Did you defraud her?" She held Bianca's gaze. "What if I contacted the Reno police, Bianca?"

"I have defrauded nobody," Bianca said through gritted teeth. "Why do you think I warned Katherine about you? The last thing I want to see is people made miserable because of frauds." She reached over and laid her hand on Katherine's. "Can you see what she's doing, Katherine? Planting seeds of doubt in your mind; preparing the ground for her to take my place."

"It's not a competition, Bianca." Georgie removed her hands, growing ever hotter, from the crystal ball. *Nerida. Elizabeth, Elizabeth, Nerida, ELIZ-ABETH.* The two names kept resounding in her mind, with flashing images of Bianca and the red-haired woman.

"Oh," she said, suddenly getting it. "*You* were Nerida, weren't you? If I searched for a medium named Nerida in Reno and matched the name with Elizabeth…would I find something?" she was watching Bianca closely as she spoke and knew she'd had a hit. "Yes, you were Nerida."

Going on the defensive, Bianca focused on Katherine. "Now you can see, Katherine, why I operate through referrals only. I know what it is to be the victim of a smear campaign, and I never want it to happen again." She stood up, looking every inch the martyr, and walked over to throw open the door. "I will have to ask you all to leave. I can't work with those who doubt me."

Georgie stayed where she was. "Have you given money to Bianca, Katherine?"

Katherine looked guilty and shot a look at Nick. "Not much."

Nick looked from her to Bianca and scowled. "What's 'not much'?"

"I sold a few things," Katherine said defensively. "I wanted to do it. Bianca takes on so few clients, but she offered to give me more regular consultations the minute she knew I was in danger. She *cares*."

"Sold what?" Nick sat straighter in his chair, and suddenly the room seemed much smaller.

"Oh, just a bit of my mother's old jewelry. I never wore it anyway."

"Oh, *Mom*. That was our emergency fallback. How much?"

"Nick, I'm your mother," Katherine said crossly. "Don't question me like this."

"Yes, well, I'm the one who has to worry all the time about the bills being paid," he shot back, furious. "Uncle Ron said last time that he wouldn't bail us out again. Do you know how much we owe?"

Georgie had kept a wary eye on Bianca, who was still managing to look insulted, but the panic beneath was surging and desperate.

She was going to run. Georgie knew it beyond all doubt.

"Hang on, Nick." Slowly, with all three of the others watching her, she wrapped up the crystal ball and put it away. "I think we all should go. Bianca has nothing more for us today. Except, perhaps, the money that Katherine has paid her." She stood up and faced Bianca. "You know the game is up, Bianca. Give it back."

"You're talking utter nonsense."

Georgie held her gaze.

Finally, the other woman gave way but remained defiant.

"You're misjudging me. I would never, never take money from someone who didn't want to give it freely. Take it! I'm happy to give it back." She stormed over to a small desk and threw open the drawer, and stood there for a moment sorting through notes before striding across to Katherine and shoving the money at her. "It's all there."

Georgie half expected Katherine to refuse it, but her face was beginning to show doubt. She took the money and stared down at it and didn't protest when Nick took it from her hands.

He riffled through it, counting swiftly. "Two and a half grand. *Mom*. You let it happen again!"

"Don't say anything." She put her head in her hands.

Georgie went over and urged her to her feet. "Come on, Katherine. Time to go."

Nick helped her, looking grim. When they reached the door, Georgie thrust the bag with the crystal ball at him. "Here. Hold this, and don't drop it."

She reached into her pocket for her phone, and

with a quick movement, activated the camera. Before Bianca had time to react, she had captured a photo of her in full sunlight.

There. That was a much clearer image for the police than the shadowy photo on the book cover.

CHAPTER 15

Nick the Rock

It appeared that Bianca-slash-Nerida had managed to cover her tracks well, because they couldn't find out anything online about a redhead named Elizabeth being involved in a psychic scam in Reno. However, a return visit to Bianca's place late the following afternoon showed that the bird had already flown.

"No sign of Bianca," Georgie reported to the others when she and Scott returned. "Just an empty apartment and one very annoyed landlady. She's been giving Bianca a deal on the rent in exchange for readings."

"I'm sure she's got plenty of cash to start again," Tammy said. "Katherine wouldn't be her only mark. And speaking of Katherine…what did she say?"

Georgie sighed. "She's pretty humiliated. This is the third time she's been sucked in by a scam artist. Imagine, three times. Nick's being a rock." She laughed. "Would you believe, after the way he was ready to call the police on me, he's now using me as a shining example to his Mom that there is good in the world. So I struck a deal: Katherine can call or email me if she has a question—free of charge, of course—and stay away from everyone else."

"That's all very well," Tammy said, "but Bianca gets away with it again!"

"Maybe not for long. Nick's on the warpath. He's put up a warning page online with the photo I took and their story, plus her Bianca-slash-Nerida aliases. He posted to the forum, too, and he plans to go to the police this time. Somehow, I don't think it'll be as easy for her to get away with it in the future."

"Well." Layla looked at the sun, low in the sky. "I guess it's Happy Hour time again. A toast to Crystal Ball Investigations? I have to say, I enjoyed driving the chase car."

"I think it's called a tail," Tammy observed, fetching glasses for the last of Scott's wine. "And I'm in a beer mood today. I've still got some of the craft beer I bought for Jerry. It's time I drank it."

The mention of Jerry had Georgie sitting bolt upright. "Oh, gosh. I forgot. Tams, I have a message for you."

"Jerry? Not interested. Thought he'd try that." Tammy carefully poured the beer so it had a perfect foaming collar. "Been rejecting his calls for days."

"That's what he said." Georgie passed the phone over. "But I think you'll want to see this one."

She watched Tammy, holding her breath. She veered from thinking that Tammy was too good for Jerry to wanting to see her happy again, and if her rat fink brother Jerry was the only thing that made Tammy come alive…well, who could fathom the ways of the universe?

Tammy paged through the photos, her face unreadable. Then she handed the phone back. "Huh." She lifted the glass of beer and sipped daintily.

Georgie exchanged looks with Layla and Scott.

Then Tammy peered at them over the rim of her glass, and a huge grin split her face. "Georgie, we won!"

Georgie lifted her wine glass in acknowledgment and grinned back. "We did."

Layla caught on immediately. "He's moved vintage trailers back?"

"Nope," Tammy said. "He's moved them to a *better* spot. The one I suggested in the first place. He's juggled everything."

"I gather he's forgiven, then," Scott observed. "That's a relief. Things were getting uncomfortable around here." He picked through Jerry's craft beer and selected one. "I'd better get my share of this before he gets back."

Georgie, Layla, and Tammy all exchanged more smiles, all perfectly in accord.

"Oh no," Tammy said, "he's got a lot of ground to make up yet. I can't be bought off that easily. I'll keep him at a distance until he learns his lesson." She stared dreamily at her treasured retro trailer, clearly planning all kinds of retribution.

Georgie stretched luxuriously. She didn't mind the sound of that. No more Jerry—at least for a while. No more threat of banishment to a corner for her vintage trailers. And no more Bianca-the-fake-psychic messing up people's lives.

Good riddance to all of them!

A NOTE FROM THE AUTHOR

I hope you enjoyed reading about Georgie's encounter with a dissatisfied jock in this story! I had a great deal of fun writing it. (Especially the scenes with Tammy. She's a girl after my own heart.)

In our next story, *Up to No Good*, Jerry gets into a whole lotta trouble—and of course Georgie helps Tammy to get him out of it!

An invitation for you: subscribe to my newsletter to get news of new releases, bonus books, specials and a sneak peek at scenes from my books in progress. As a welcome gift, you'll also receive a copy of *Fortune's Wheel*, the prequel to the Georgie series.

Here's your chance to find out more about the intriguing old woman that Georgie sees as a kind of taciturn genie. Whether she wanted to believe it or not, from birth Georgie was destined to follow in Great-Grandma Rosa's footsteps—as well as inherit her crystal ball!

If you haven't already done so, visit my website below to join other readers and download your copy.

MargMcAlister.com/free-georgie-book/

ABOUT THE AUTHOR

Marg McAlister is the author of the popular Georgie B. Goode Cozy Mystery series (set in the USA) and Series 2 (Australian RV Adventure series), also featuring Georgie.

Marg lives by the sea on the mid-north coast of NSW, but she and her husband spend part of the year on The Gemfields in Central Queensland, living off the grid on their mining claim. While her husband digs for sapphires and zircons, operates the wash plant and drives around dirt tracks, Marg is usually writing—or socializing!

Marg is also the author of a series of books for aspiring writers, and the owner of Blue Gem Publishing, which publishes books in a range of genres.

Next in This Series
UP TO NO GOOD

Excerpt

Georgie sat with her chin resting on her hand, frowning at her crystal ball. She should have been a hacker instead of a fortuneteller. Hackers could dig deep and find out people's deepest, darkest secrets with much more certainty than staring into a stupid crystal ball.

Being a wizard could work, too. *Schazam*, wave a wand and demand answers from… well, somebody. Or maybe to have messages from beyond arrive via owl post, like Harry Potter.

"Will I marry and have children?"

"Give me a second; an owl will be along any second now with the answer."

She reached over and smoothed a hand over the gleaming surface of the crystal ball and then gave it a light tap. "Come *on*. What's going on with you?"

For two weeks now, her crystal ball had been acting up—if that was the correct term to use with something that didn't plug into a wall. Her customers still seemed entertained enough—but there was some kind of severe blockage in the channel.

Did you even *call* it a channel?

Georgie groaned and banged her head gently on the table. She was such a know-nothing. A couple of months of success had made her over-confident; that was the problem. She had expected her understanding of all this to grow, and instead, she had gone backward. So much for being an eighth-generation gypsy who had supposedly inherited the Sight.

What had happened to the strange drifting white mist that had scared her to death the first time she used the crystal ball? It was gone.

Gone.

Find it at your preferred bookstore or online:
https://books2read.com/Up-To-No-Good